ISBN: 979-8-89324-958-3

Published by Franklin Publishers

Printed in the United States of America

For permissions, inquiries, or additional copies, contact:

Franklin Publishers

www.franklinpublishers.com

Table of Contents

Prologue

The town was too perfect. Streetlamps glowed with soft amber light, illuminating identical houses packed together like teeth. Each home, compact and pristine, stood at precise angles — not a blade of grass out of place, not a window left ajar. It looked less like a neighborhood and more like a display — a model town, built more for symmetry than soul.

It didn't look lived in.

It looked arranged.

Beyond the last row of homes, the world began to rot.

Dense fog rolled in off the black lake that ringed the town like a moat, thick and heavy, carrying the faint reek of algae and iron. The water barely moved, its surface glassy, reflecting the streetlights in trembling smears. Somewhere in that gray distance came a low, hungry sound — too big, too wild to belong anywhere near a place like this.

A moving truck sat parked in the driveway of one such house — a modest two-story painting of a sterile shade of beige. Boxes were stacked high on the porch, still taped shut, waiting for morning. Inside, the air was thick with dust and plastic. Furniture sat half-unwrapped beneath cloudy sheeting, ghostly shapes in the dim light. Every room echoed with that transitional emptiness — a house not yet claimed, not yet alive.

In the master bedroom, Anna sat upright in bed, the glow of her phone painting her face in ghostly blue. She scrolled through her inbox with slow, mechanical flicks of her thumb — Welcome to the neighborhood. Important

HOA notice. Your security code. Each subject line made her stomach twist tighter.

"You sure everything's going to be okay overnight?" she asked, glancing toward the half-open bathroom door. Her voice tried to be calm. "I hate that we didn't finish unpacking. It just feels… off."

From the bathroom, Jesse spoke around a mouthful of toothpaste.

"Part of the sales pitch was the town's twenty-four-hour patrol," he said, spitting into the sink. "We're good."

He stared at his reflection for a long moment. The fluorescent light buzzed overhead, flickering once, drawing his attention to the blank window beyond. He rubbed his face hard, trying to shake the feeling that had crept in during the drive — that strange pressure behind the eyes, like he was a specimen in a museum, being watched through perfect, unbroken glass.

"We have provided security," he muttered again. The words didn't sound like comfort. They sounded like a lie he wanted to believe. "Of course it'll be okay."

Then came the crash.

It exploded through the house like a gunshot — the unmistakable sound of breaking glass, splintering wood, and something heavy hitting the floor.

Jesse froze. For a heartbeat, he just stared at himself in the mirror, breath held, listening. Then he stepped back from the sink, heart kicking up, and moved toward the bedroom.

"I'm going to check that out," he said softly, already halfway across the room. His voice was steady, but his pulse wasn't.

Anna looked up, worry etched into her features. "Be careful," she whispered.

The stairs groaned beneath him as he descended, phone held out like a flashlight. Each step creaked sharply and loudly against the silence. At the bottom, the beam caught the front door — shattered inward. Glass glittered across the floor like frost.

Cold air rushed in, curling around his ankles. The night felt wrong and alive.

Jesse stepped carefully through the wreckage. The crunch of broken glass was loud underfoot despite his best efforts. His phone light caught a glow ahead — the refrigerator door, hanging open, humming faintly. Its pale light spilled across the tile in a perfect rectangle.

He moved closer.

Something shifted in the shadows.

Jesse froze mid-step. The air carried a sound — a low, wet breathing, rhythmic and heavy, like an animal feeding. He took one cautious step forward, then another, heart pounding against his ribs like it wanted out.

From the doorway, he could just make out the thing hunched over the fridge — broad shoulders rising and falling. The light caught fur: black, matted, and wet. Clawed paws. Muscular haunches.

Then it lifted its head.

The wolf — if it was a wolf — was massive, almost counter-height. Its eyes glowed with a faint, hellish red, as if lit from within. Strips of meat hung from its jaws, slick with blood.

Jesse didn't breathe.

Then it saw him.

"Jesse?" Anna's voice cut through the stillness like a blade.

His eyes widened. "Anna, no—shut up," he hissed, the words barely clearing his throat.

The creature's ears twitched.

It turned fully now, massive head rising.

Then came the sound — click click click — claws on hardwood.

Jesse turned and ran.

He took the stairs two at a time, bounding as fast as his legs could carry him, skipping every other tread. He reached the landing and made for the bedroom, but the pounding of paws behind him was impossibly fast.

The impact drove him backward into the wall. His breath exploded from his chest. He barely had time to raise an arm before the jaws opened wide—

There was no time to scream.

Then everything went red.

Blood sprayed the room in great arcs, splattering the ceiling, the walls. The sound was wet and final.

Anna couldn't move. She listened, frozen, as the thing fed — the steady rhythm of tearing and chewing, almost calm.

"Jesse?" she whispered. Her voice broke on the name.

The creature fed — grunting, chewing, tearing muscles and tendon with methodical hunger. Each sound was more unbearable than the last.

Something inside her broke.

Anna bolted from the bed, her scream trapped behind her teeth. Her feet slid — not on water, but on a slick, awful layer of fresh blood flooding the hall, hands clawing for the stair frame. The creature lunged — missing her by inches — and slammed into the wall with a roar that rattled the windows.

She tumbled down the stairs, slamming hard onto the ground floor. Broken glass tore into her skin — legs, palms, arms — but she kept crawling, blood smearing across the tile in frantic streaks. She dragged herself through the doorway, out into the freezing night air.

"Help me! Please!"

Across the street, a man watched from his window in a haunting glow.

"Help! Please!"

He met her gaze through the glass — expression blank, unmoving. Then, slowly, he reached up and closed the curtain. The house went dark.

"No… no, no, please—"

Anna ran barefoot into the street, blood slicked on her skin. Porch lights blinked on one by one — only to die out again as she passed. Curtains drawn. Locks clicking into place.

Her screams echoed through the neighborhood, but the town stayed silent.

She stumbled and fell, continuing to push herself up to keep running.

Behind her, the heavy sound of paws followed. Closer. Closer.

She didn't look back — not until she felt the heat of it behind her, its breath on her neck.

She turned, smearing blood from her face, and looked up.

Two red eyes hovered in the dark, burning low like embers.

She opened her mouth to scream—

And the darkness swallowed her whole.

8

Silence returned to Pine Lakes slowly, like a door easing shut.

For a long moment, nothing moved.

Then, from between the houses, shapes emerged.

Small ones.

They stepped out of alleys and side yards, six… eight… more… their outlines thin and child-sized, their bodies swallowed in dark, hooded garments that brushed the ground. They moved with an eerie, practiced unity — no chatter, no hesitation, no fear.

Only purpose.

The wolf waited in the center of the street, panting, muzzle dripping. One of the shadows approached it, head bowed. A soft, chittering whisper passed between them, too quiet to make out. The wolf lowered itself, almost obedient, then turned and vanished between the houses, disappearing into the backyard darkness.

The shadows got to work.

Two dragged Jesse's limp remains down the staircase by the wrists, leaving a red smear along the steps. Others slipped into the bedroom, gathering stray pieces of him in small metal bins they carried like lunch pails.

Another group followed Anna's trail, sweeping the street with wide, jointed brooms that made no sound at all.

Wherever their tools passed, blood vanished — dissolved, absorbed, erased.

A taller shadow — taller than the rest but still hunched — paused at the curb, turning its head toward the lake. Listening.

When it spoke, its voice was papery and thin.

"Before dawn."

The others nodded — a single, synchronized movement — and continued their work.

Within minutes, the house was silent.
Within fifteen, it was spotless.
Within twenty, Pine Lakes looked perfect again.

Just another beautiful town with nothing at all wrong beneath the surface.

Chapter One

Steam hissed from beneath the hood of a dusty green Jeep parked on the shoulder of a long, sun-bleached Alabama highway. The late afternoon air was thick and unmoving, cicadas buzzing lazily from the trees. Heat shimmered across the asphalt in waves.

A young man leaned against the front fender, his right hand in a purple cast, tapping restlessly against the metal. His skin glistened with sweat. He squinted toward the horizon, where pine trees crowded the edges of the road like silent sentries.

"Where are we?" Todd asked, his voice dry with irritation.

From beneath the car, a low grunt answered. "Somewhere between Mobile and Montgomery."

A pair of grease-streaked legs slid out from under the Jeep. George — older, weathered, and visibly exhausted — wiped his hands on his already-filthy cargo pants and pushed himself upright.

Todd stared at him, arms crossed. "Remind me again. Why are we in Alabama?"

George shrugged, squinting at the engine. "Me? For work. You? Because of stupid decisions."

Todd narrowed his eyes. He slammed the hood shut, harder than necessary.

"Don't be a bitch about it," George muttered, rounding the front of the vehicle.

"I lost my internship. I worked hard for that," Todd snapped. "It wasn't just—"

"—One mistake?" George finished, cutting him off. "It's never just one. Don't pretend you didn't drag yourself into the mess."

He got into the car and turned the key. The engine roared back to life with a rattling that sounded like it might not last the day.

"And now," he added, "you get to work for me. Call it penance. Or hell. Your choice. I'll even show you how I fix the car."

George shut the hood with a grunt and wiped sweat from his forehead. "Before we get trapped on the side of the road again," he said, "we're stopping for gas."

They drove another ten minutes before a lonely gas station appeared on the right — a squat, concrete building with peeling green paint and a flickering fluorescent sign that read PINE STOP. The place looked abandoned except for a single red vending machine humming weakly beside the door.

George pulled in next to pump three.

"Grab us some drinks," he said. "And don't steal anything. I'm too old to outrun a clerk today."

Todd rolled his eyes but stepped out of the Jeep, the heat slamming into him like a wall. The cicadas were louder here. Too loud.

The bell above the door jingled as he pushed inside.

The place smelled like old mop water and lemon cleaner. Rows of snacks sat in perfect lines, unbothered by dust or fingerprints. The air was freezing, unnaturally so, like someone had kept the AC on high even at night.

Behind the counter stood two teenagers — twins, by the look of them.

Same height. Same haircut. Same too-wide eyes.

They didn't turn to greet him.

They were already staring.

Todd froze mid-step. "Uh… hi."

Both twins blinked. Slowly. Perfectly in sync.

"Hello," they said together.

Todd swallowed and grabbed two bottles of water from the cooler. When he shut the door, the glass rattled — and both twins flinched violently, like the sound was too sharp.

He stepped to the counter and set the bottles down.

"Just these."

The twin on the left leaned forward.

"You headed somewhere?"

"Yeah," Todd said. "Going to Pine Lakes."

Both twins went rigid.

Right Twin tapped the counter with one finger — fast, nervous.

Left Twin glanced toward the door.

"You shouldn't go there," Right Twin whispered.

Todd frowned. "Why not?"

Left Twin swallowed.

"People go in sometimes… but Pine Lakes doesn't always let them leave."

Todd tried to laugh. "Cool. Great tourist slogan."

Neither blinked.

Right Twin leaned closer.

"You'll see things there. You'll think they're normal. They're not."

Left Twin nodded.

"Don't go near the lake at night."

Todd shifted, uncomfortable. "We're…my dad is writing a thing."

Both twins shared a slow, mournful look — something like pity.

Finally, Right Twin slid the water bottles back.

"That'll be four bucks."

Todd paid, but Right Twin didn't take the money right away.
He stared at Todd's cast, voice soft:

"You hurt?"

"Yeah," Todd muttered. "Long story."

Right Twin nodded once.

"Don't make it longer."

Todd didn't breathe again until he stepped back into the heat.

The twins kept staring through the window long after the bell stopped ringing.

Todd circled to the passenger side and yanked at the door. It was stuck. Of course it did. With an annoyed grunt, he reached through the open window and unlocked it manually. The door creaked open, protesting being disturbed.

"So, we're here for one of your stories?" he asked, sliding into the seat and slamming the door.

George glanced at him, one brow raised. "Been digging into this for months. People go missing. Money disappears. Then nobody talks. A few rich families started asking questions. I think the answers are buried in a place called Pine Lakes."

Todd snorted. "You judge my shitty life decisions, then drag me into a Scooby-Doo mystery. Cool."

"You're welcome." George smiled as he put on his sunglasses.

They pulled back onto the road, the Jeep rattling as it picked up speed. The highway ahead narrowed, winding through dense forest. Trees leaned overhead, thick with moss and shadow, until the sky all but disappeared.

Todd sighed and threw his legs up onto the dashboard, his boot knocking loose a piece of cracked plastic. "Let's move to the spooky town," he muttered.

George grinned. "Atta boy."

The Jeep rounded a final bend in the road — and just like that, the forest peeled away.

The transition was instant.

Where thick trees had lined the highway, now there was only open space. A shallow valley spread below them, framed by low hills and tall pines. Nestled in the heart of it was a town that looked untouched by time: narrow streets, identical houses packed together like teeth. Each home, compact and pristine, stood at precise angles.

A wooden sign stood crooked at the roadside, hand-carved letters painted in fading white:

WELCOME TO PINE LAKES.

Todd turned in his seat, glancing behind them.

The highway was gone.

Not just receding into the distance — gone. The road they'd traveled on had been violently severed, swallowed by thick trees and a sudden, impenetrable mist. Where asphalt had been, now there was only dense forest and a stillness that tasted like a dead end.

He turned back toward the windshield, pulse quickening.

"What the hell was that? Did you see that?" he asked.

George was staring ahead, wide-eyed. "Yeah," he whispered. "Amazing. I've only seen a few pictures. But I get it now. Though I still don't understand why people move here. Twenty disappearances in twenty-five years — and that's just what's been reported."

Todd kept his eyes on the town as they descended into the valley. "Dead people really bring out the best in you, huh?"

George shrugged. "It's not about the dead. It's about the story. And this one's buried under layers of silence."

As they passed the first few houses, Todd noticed the details: everyone smiled. Families waved from their porches. Children rode bikes in perfectly spaced intervals. A man grilled hot dogs in a driveway, flipping them with casual perfection. There was no traffic. No trash. Not even a dog barking.

The town was too clean.

"You're telling me the police looked into all this?" Todd asked.

"They claimed to," George said. "But the files get closed. No follow-up. No answers. The chief at the time retired early and now runs a bait shop in Gulf Shores."

"Classic."

They passed a freshly painted community center, where a sign read **FAMILY PICNIC: SATURDAY @ 5 PM – DON'T MISS IT!** A group of teens played cornhole on the lawn, waving as the Jeep drove by.

Todd gave a tight smile but didn't wave back. "Are all the residents wealthy?" he asked instead.

"You'd have to be. The cost of living here is absurd. Most of the money comes from old southern families — oil, timber, land. Our great-uncle's moonshine business paid for this trip, and your recent rehab stay, by the way."

Todd sighed. "Nothing says support like bringing it up every five minutes."

George ignored the jab. "People here act like nothing's wrong. But there's close to twenty million dollars in unaccounted assets from the missing. No digital trail. No family inheritance. Just... gone."

Todd's fingers tapped restlessly on his cast. "Let me guess: cult? Serial killer? Freddy Krueger? Maybe the lake's haunted."

George smirked. "No comment. Yet. But a haunted lake would be pretty cool."

They turned a corner, and for the first time, Todd saw it — the lake itself. Deep and glassy, it sat at the far edge of town like a secret. Mist curled along its surface despite the heat, and behind it loomed a massive church perched on a ridge, dark and towering, its steeple like a finger pointing at the sky.

Todd stared, unease crawling up the back of his neck.

As they passed a row of houses, more residents waved. Some stood motionless at the edge of their lawns, smiling too widely. Their eyes followed the Jeep as it moved past — unblinking.

George didn't notice.

Todd leaned closer to the window, brow furrowed.

"Why do they all keep watching us?"

George didn't answer.

Not because he didn't hear.

Because he didn't want to.

Chapter Two

The sun hung high over Pine Lakes, painting the street in thick, syrupy gold. Heat rippled off the pavement, bending the air like water. A lone cicada droned in the distance as George and Todd hauled boxes from the trailer pulled by the Jeep, its tires finally resting after the long journey.

The house, calm and pristine, looked as though it had never been lived in. Its white trim looked freshly painted, and its shutters were scrubbed clean. The porch swing creaked softly in the breeze, even though no one had touched it.

Across the road, a man sat in a lawn chair, still as a statue in a museum. Short-sleeved flannel. Khaki shorts. One hand around a sweating glass of lemonade. The other rested motionless on his thigh. He didn't even pretend not to stare.

Todd set down a box and squinted. "He's been watching us since we pulled in."

George didn't look up from the dolly. "So, wave."

"Wave? I can't tell if he's welcoming us or casing the place."

"Be nice," George muttered, wheeling the dolly toward the porch.

Todd raised a hand in a half-hearted salute. The man across the street stood slowly, stretched, and began crossing the road with a relaxed gait—like someone who'd never hurried a day in his life.

"Great," Todd muttered. "He's coming over. Cue the exposition."

The man walked like someone who had never lived anywhere else. Like the town had carved a space inside him and stayed there, he reached the end of the driveway and extended his hand with practiced warmth.

"Hi there! I'm Jack—your new neighbor. Welcome to Pine Lakes."

George stepped forward and shook his hand. It was firm, dry, and confident. "George Webb. This is my son, Todd."

Todd gave a polite nod from behind a stack of boxes.

Jack looked toward the house with a hint of wistful nostalgia. "You're gonna love this place. The last folks took great care of it, shame they couldn't stay longer. The garden's a little wild, but the bones are good."

George followed his gaze. "Looks that way. We are excited to settle in after a drive like ours and be lazy for a bit."

Jack chuckled. "If lazy's what you're after, I've got a grill full of meat and no self-control. I'll bring some by tonight, so you don't have to cook."

Todd peeked from behind the truck. "Something that's not pie? That'll be a first."

George smirked. "We've had, what, eight pies today?"

"Nine," Todd said. "The one with the fancy crust showed up while you were unloading that last load."

Jack laughed. "Yeah, some of the ladies compete. Some of the men, too—they just won't admit it."

As if summoned by the words, a woman approached from the sidewalk in a flowing pastel sundress, heels tapping rhythmically. She carried a pie wrapped in a neatly folded cloth. Her skin was glowing in the sunlight as if it had been airbrushed. Her smile was the kind that never quite reached the eyes.

20

"Hello, new neighbors!" she called. "Hi, Jack—are you making us look good?"

Jack turned, greeting her with a side hug. "Just doing my part. And look at that—another pie."

He clapped George on the shoulder. "Pleasure meeting you both. I'll see you tonight with the good stuff."

"Looking forward to it," George nodded.

The woman stepped closer. "I'm Maria," she said, offering the pie. "I work for the Mayor. He sends his apologies. He got tied up in a meeting and will be along shortly."

George accepted the dish with a smile. "George Webb. Nice to meet you."

Todd jumped down from the truck, wiping sweat from his forehead. "We've only been here a few hours, and it's starting to feel like we're running a bakery."

Maria laughed. "We take hospitality seriously in Pine Lakes. You must be Todd."

He raised an eyebrow. "That obvious?"

"It's in the posture," she teased. "And the cast. That looks like a story waiting to be told."

George smiled faintly as Todd disappeared inside with the pie.

"Everyone's been kind," George said. "Maybe a little too kind."

Maria tilted her head. "Too kind? That's not something we hear often."

George's tone was casual, but his eyes lingered on her just a second longer than they should have. "Just a writer's instinct, I guess. Always looking for cracks in the surface to turn into another story."

Her smile stayed fixed, but her gaze cooled. "Some surfaces are meant to shine."

George gestured toward the porch. "Join me?"

They climbed the steps and settled into a pair of chairs beneath the eaves. The air was warm, but the shade brought a small relief.

Todd reappeared with plates and a fork for each of them.

George lifted a slice. "Here's to second chances."

He took a bite — and paused.

The flavor was deep, layered — apples, yes, but something else too. Something darker, with a hint of spice and soil, like autumn buried in the crust. It tasted like a memory.

Maria sat quietly now, watching the road. Her smile had faded.

George followed her gaze.

A man emerged from the trees across the street. Slender. Dressed in a suit jacket that fluttered despite the still air. The shadows of the branches clung to him like smoke. When he turned toward them, George caught a flash of his face—angular features, precise, as if he'd been carved out of light and polished to a shine.

Maria stood. "There's the Mayor now."

George rose beside her as the man approached, the last of the shadows sliding away.

"George!" the man boomed, all teeth and charm. "So glad to finally meet you. Mayor Donald Merrick—but folks call me Donald. Or Mayor. I like it too much to correct them."

His handshake was warm. His presence was heavier than it should've been.

"Pleasure, Donald," George said. "The pie's... fantastic."

Todd stepped outside.

Donald turned, smiling widely. "You must be Todd. Glad I caught you before the day got away from us."

Todd nodded politely. "Nice to meet you, sir."

"We're thrilled to have you both. Not everyday Pine Lakes gets a real novelist moving into town."

Todd blinked. "He's a good storyteller; I'll give him that."

George shot his son a look, careful but sharp. "That's kind of you to say," he told the Mayor.

Donald chuckled. "You'll find there's plenty to inspire you here. Small towns are full of stories. Ours just happen to have happy endings."

"They can't all be happy," George said, with a chuckle

Donald's smile didn't falter. "Oh, we have our drama. We just keep it where it belongs—quietly managed."

Maria adjusted her dress. "We should let you two finish up. Don't work too hard."

Todd gave a lazy salute. "As soon as this trailer's empty, I plan never to lift another thing again."

Donald clasped George's hand once more. "This is your town now, too. If you need anything — anything at all — Maria and I are always around. As are your neighbors. You'll find people here who go out of their way to make you feel at home. Hospitality isn't a slogan — it's a promise."

He and Maria walked down the road, their silhouettes swallowed by the golden haze. The shadows along the sidewalk seemed to sway as they passed, and when they were gone, the street returned to its previous hush.

Inside, the front door clicked shut behind Todd.

Boxes towered in the living room, throwing long cardboard shadows.

Todd turned to George. "A novelist? Really?"

George didn't look up from unpacking. "People talk less around writers. They assume you're harmless."

Todd stared. "Jesus, Dad. Couldn't you just say you were a retired journalist? Something that doesn't make us sound like we're here to write the next Twin Peaks?"

George smirked. "I told them the truth."

Todd leaned on the doorway. "Which truth? That I'm a brilliant young photographer who just got a little too excited at a company party? Or the one where I got canned, spiraled, and landed in rehab because I couldn't tell the difference between adrenaline and addiction?"

George walked into the kitchen and grabbed another fork.

"The rehab truth," he said. "The other version's still a little spicy for polite conversation. People around here will find out eventually. Best they hear it from us — neat and packaged."

Todd crossed his arms. "You're a terrible father."

George pointed the fork. "Terrible fathers don't bring their kids to towns filled with pie and perfect people. That's Grade-A parenting."

He took a bite and sighed contentedly.

"That is a damn good pie."

Todd rolled his eyes and wandered back into the living room. He opened a battered box labeled **DO NOT BREAK, OR MOM WILL HAUNT YOU** and lifted an old game board.

"Is that Risk?" George called out.

Todd held it up. "Yeah. You still have this?"

"Your mother never let me throw it out," George said as he tossed a box down the hallway.

Todd carried the game toward the hallway.

He took two steps onto the first stair before something crunched under his boot.

Todd paused.

The sound wasn't like cardboard or old house settling. It was… sharper.

He lifted his foot.

A sliver of something pale lay on the stair tread — thin, curved, almost translucent. At first glance, it looked like part of a broken ornament. But when he picked it up between his fingers, he felt the slight give of organic material.

A toenail?

No — too thick. Too long.

Goosebumps prickled up his neck.

He set the game on the banister and leaned down, inspecting the stair frame more closely. That's when he saw it:

Claw marks.

Faint, but deep — three vertical gouges carved into the white-painted wood. The grooves were spaced far apart, wider than any dog should leave. Someone had painted over them, but the paint hadn't fully filled the trenches. Under the afternoon light, the grooves cast tiny shadows.

Todd ran his thumb along the deepest cut.

Not old.

Not brand new either.

But recent enough to raise every alarm in his body.

He looked farther down the hallway. Near the baseboard, the paint warped — a subtle pattern he hadn't noticed earlier. Todd crouched, running his fingers over it. The paint bubbled in spots as if it had been laid over water damage… except when he pressed on it lightly, it cracked.

A reddish-black smear appeared beneath.

Todd jerked his hand back.

Blood.

Old, but not old-old.

Maybe a few weeks. Maybe less.

A shiver crawled down his spine.

He glanced back toward the living room, where George sat at the table, eating Maria's pie like nothing existed outside the kitchen window.

Todd swallowed dryly and slowly rose.

He made his way farther down the hall, almost against his own will. The air felt different here — cooler, heavier. He reached the end of the hall and turned toward the master bedroom doorway.

Another mark waited there.

Not a claw mark this time.

A dent.
About shoulder-height.
Plaster cracked outward, as if something had been thrown into the wall hard enough to deform it.

Todd rested his fingers over the spot.

Something bad happened here.

Something violent.

Something the realtor sure as hell hadn't mentioned.

Behind him, a floorboard creaked — but the house didn't feel empty.
It felt like it was holding its breath.

"Todd!" George called from the living room, breaking the spell. "Where are you headed?"

Todd pulled back from the wall like he'd been caught doing something wrong. He snatched up the Risk board, cleared his throat, and forced lightness into his voice.

"Just looking for a place to put this," he lied.

His hand trembled slightly as he climbed the stairs.

Chapter Three

Todd sat alone in his room, amber light from the desk lamp casting crooked shadows across cardboard boxes and half-assembled furniture. The space still felt foreign—like a hotel room someone had hastily decorated to mimic home.

His camera gear was the only part of him fully unpacked—lenses gleaming, tripod standing like a sentry near the window. A low hum rose from his laptop as it chewed through high-resolution images.

Classical music whispered from an open browser tab—Bach, maybe. Something restrained. It contrasted sharply with the knotted anxiety in his chest.

He clicked through photos from their drive south: cracked highways, blurred treetops, the fading blue of dusk in the rearview mirror. One image froze him—George leaning against the Jeep, cigarette tucked behind his ear, shirt streaked with engine grease. Todd zoomed in on his own reflection in the side mirror—his cast still a clean bright purple, not yet stained with dirt and roadside grit.

Across the room, the RISK board sat frozen mid-battle. Plastic armies paused in eternal war.

And then—

A scream.

Loud. Wet. Raw.

It sliced through the stillness like a blade, sharp and immediate.

Todd froze. His breath caught in his throat, eyes jerking away from the screen. The sound evaporated almost as quickly as it came, replaced by a silence so heavy it rang in his ears. A second noise followed—a long, low howl. Not a dog. Not a coyote. Something... deeper. Something sad and primal.

Todd whispered, "What the hell was that?"

He stood slowly, instinct warring with curiosity. The floorboards creaked beneath him as he crossed to the window. He parted the curtain just enough to see. The trees were there, still and ordinary—but something moved among them. A shadow darker than the darkness, gliding just out of sight.

Another howl.
Closer this time.

He didn't hesitate. He grabbed his camera and slung the strap around his neck like armor.

The house was deathly still. George lay passed out on the couch, snoring beside a half-spilled beer and an open notebook labeled Working Title: Pines and Shadows.

Todd hovered over him.
"I thought that it was you out there," he whispered.

No response. Just a snore.

He nudged George's shoulder. "Hey. Wake up."

Todd sighed. "Cool. I'll let you know what happens," he muttered, pulling open the front door.

Fog greeted him like breath from a giant mouth—thick and wet and immediate. The world outside had softened at the edges, detail swallowed by haze. Porch lights blurred into pale halos. The ground sloped gently down toward the treeline, the shed's bulb buzzing weakly in the distance like an old man trying to speak.

Todd moved slowly, camera raised. His sneakers sank into the grass with a damp squish. The trees didn't move, but something between them did—gliding in rhythm with his heartbeat.

Then came the sound.

A snap.

A crunch.

The unmistakable wet tear of meat.

Todd froze. "Oh, shove off," he hissed under his breath. "Is anyone else hearing this shit?"

He crept forward, cautiously, heart pounding. He could feel it again—that sensation from the highway as if the world had shifted sideways. Like Pine Lakes wasn't just a place, but a threshold.

And then—

It leapt.

A black shape burst from the treeline.

The wolf landed with the weight of a boulder. Its eyes burned like dying stars. Blood dripped from its muzzle, steaming in the fog. The creature was impossibly large, all muscle and malice, its fur like obsidian daggers under the light.

Todd screamed and stumbled backward, his cast slamming into the ground. The breath left his lungs in a sharp burst as the camera skidded across the grass.

The wolf didn't charge. It stalked forward, slow and deliberate like it had time. Like it had done this before.

Todd reached for the camera, his broken arm raised in defense like a weak shield.

The wolf lunged.

Pain exploded in his arm as jaws clamped onto the cast. He screamed. It felt like his bones had been caught in a trash compactor. But the cast held.

With his free hand, he managed to grab the camera and began snapping photos uncontrollably. The shutter clicked four times—fast, desperate, a machine gun of light.

Flash.

The light burst like lightning.

Flash.

Another burst. The wolf recoiled, eyes flaring, claws swiping through the air.

Flash.

It howled—pain, fury, something older. Then it turned, almost calmly, and vanished into the trees. The fog swallowed it whole.

Todd bolted. No plan. No direction. Just motion. Pure panic is driving his legs.

Todd burst through the front door like a gunshot, shoulder slamming it shut behind him. Fog clung to his clothes like ghosts.

George jolted upright on the couch, startled and half-dreaming.

"What happened? What time is it?"

Todd didn't speak. He stood panting, clutching the camera to his chest like a crucifix.

His breath hitched—just once, sharply.

George blinked twice, the last traces of sleep evaporating from his eyes. He sat up straighter, scanning Todd's face, the dirt smeared across his clothes, the tremor in his hands. The beer beside him might as well have vanished from existence. His whole posture changed—alert, sober, father.

"Todd," he said quietly, "come here."

Todd shook his head like a frightened animal. "I—I can't. I don't—Dad, I don't know what that thing—"

George was already crossing the room. He put both hands on Todd's shoulders, steadying him. Todd flinched but didn't pull away.

"You're hurt," George said. Not accusatory. Not panicked. Just a fact.

He guided Todd toward the couch, lowering him onto the cushions with care. "Let me see your arm."

Todd resisted for half a second before the adrenaline collapsed out of him. He lifted the cast with trembling fingers.

George's eyes hardened when he saw the dents—deep, fresh bite marks indented into the fiberglass.

"Jesus Christ," George breathed. "Todd… something actually bit you?"

Todd nodded, jaw clenched so tight it trembled. "It was huge. Bigger than any dog I've ever seen. It—Dad, it attacked me."

George took a knee in front of him, examining the damage with gentle hands. His movements were surprisingly delicate—quick but careful, like he'd done this a hundred times. Todd winced as George pressed near the elbow.

"I'm not broken," Todd muttered, voice cracking. "Just—shaken."

George exhaled, shoulders dropping with a mixture of relief and dread. "You scared the hell out of me."

Todd blinked hard, suddenly fighting tears he didn't want to show. "I thought it was gonna kill me. I really—Dad, I really thought—"

George didn't let him finish.
He pulled Todd into a tight, steady hug.

For a moment, Todd didn't react. His arms hung limply.

Then he let go of the breath he'd been holding since the clearing. His forehead pressed into George's shoulder.

"Jesus, Dad," he whispered shakily. "I'm not ready for this."

"I know," George said, tightening his hold. "But you're here. You made it back. That's what matters."

After a long moment, George eased him back, wiping dirt from Todd's cheek with the edge of his sleeve.

"Sit," George said gently. "Don't move. I'll get the first-aid kit."

"I'm fine," Todd muttered automatically.

George's voice dropped into the tone only fathers have mastered:
"You're bleeding, Todd. Humor me."

Todd swallowed, nodding once.

George returned with a battered metal kit and set it on the table. His hands were steady as he cleaned the scrapes on Todd's knees and arm, brushed away dried blood, and taped gauze where the skin had torn beneath the cast.

He didn't ask any more questions. Not yet.

Finally, he sat beside him on the couch.

"Todd," he said quietly, "look at me."

Todd did.

"I believe you."

That, more than anything, made Todd's throat tighten.

George nodded toward the dark window. "I don't know what you saw out there—wolf, creature, something else entirely—but you're not crazy. And you're not alone in this."

Todd stared at him, eyes burning. "…Thank you."

George clapped him gently on the back. "Now, I'm making coffee. You go to your room and upload whatever you managed to capture, and don't die. Deal?"

Todd let out a shaky laugh. "Deal."

George moved to the kitchen, already more awake than he had been all day.

He shuffled to the counter, running a hand through his hair.

"Cream or sugar?" he called softly.

Todd walked by with a weak smile. "Both."

"You got it."

The kettle hissed.

The fog pressed against the windows like a thing alive.

And for the first time since stepping into Pine Lakes—

Todd didn't feel entirely alone.

In his room, Todd dropped into the chair at his desk, shoulders hunched. The monitor's glow lit his face as he clicked through the photos—overexposed flashes, blurred fur, eyes like burning coals. Every image felt alive, crawling.

George appeared behind him, coffee in hand, rubbing his beard.
The notebook lay open on the desk—pages looping with notes about the nature of small-town secrets.

George leaned closer, squinting at the screen.
"It could be an animal," he said quietly.

Todd didn't look away. "It was an animal."

George nodded slowly. "I believe you. Especially with those teeth marks in your cast."
He paused. "But you know what we need."

"Proof," Todd said.

"Right." George set the coffee down. "People here think I'm writing a novel. Let's keep it that way. If anyone asks, you're helping me with research—photos, local color."
He exhaled through his nose. "Writers ask good questions. Folks like answering 'em."

Todd frowned. "So, the writer thing is a cover."

George shrugged. "Covers keep you alive."

He tapped the monitor gently. "But these? They're not enough yet. Tomorrow, we will play it slowly. You take more pictures. Blend in. Let the town get used to you."

Todd swallowed hard. "And if someone knows about… that thing out there?"

George hesitated.

"If you bring up the wolf, do it casually," he said. "Watch their faces. See who flinches."

Todd nodded, but his eyes stayed glued to the photos. The room felt too small. Too warm. The shadows moved with the corner of his vision.

George clapped his shoulder gently and wandered back toward the living room. "Get some sleep. We'll talk more in the morning."

Todd didn't move for a long time.

Eventually, his adrenaline drained all at once, leaving his limbs heavy and his thoughts sluggish. He closed the laptop, pulled off the camera strap with shaking hands, and kicked off his shoes.

He lay back on the bed—fully clothed—staring at the ceiling.

The house creaked around him.

A distant howl rose in the woods.

Faint.

Or maybe imagined.

His eyelids drooped.

He whispered to the quiet room, "What the hell did we just walk into?"

And then, finally—

Todd slept.

Chapter Four

The town center looked like something from a faded 1950s calendar—too perfect to be real. Brick sidewalks wove between pastel awnings. . . . Everything felt arranged. Controlled. Like a simulation running on precise, deliberate inputs. Brick sidewalks wove between pastel awnings; each storefront painted in gentle Easter tones that gleamed beneath the warm morning sun. A soft breeze drifted through the square, nudging hanging flower baskets and American flags just enough to make the place feel alive. Or like it was pretending to be.

Todd walked along the sidewalk with his camera slung across his shoulder, the shutter clicking every few steps. The town practically staged its own photos—vintage benches, trimmed hedges, a bakery storefront with pies displayed like museum artifacts. Everything felt arranged. Controlled. Curated.

People greeted him by name as if they'd known him for years.

"Morning, Todd!"

"Hey there, Mr. Webb!"

"Tell your dad we said hello!"

Each voice carried that same warm familiarity—just off enough to make his stomach twist.

How the hell does everyone know who I am?

He managed polite nods, but his grip tightened around the camera strap. Even the sunlight felt too bright, like stage lighting.

Crossing the street with a sandwich George had shoved at him earlier, Todd drifted into a small park beside the square. The grass was perfectly clipped, the fountain water impossibly clear, as if Pine Lakes hadn't experienced a real storm in decades.

Todd lifted his camera again, snapping a shot of an elderly man sweeping the front of the hardware store. It was a beautiful shot—sunlight, dust motes, the old man's silhouette framed beneath the awning.

Click.

Click.

On the third photo, the broom paused mid-sweep.

The old man slowly lifted his head.

His eyes were wrong—flat, glassy, like buttons sewn too tight.

"You shouldn't take pictures of people without their say-so," he said.

Todd blinked. "Oh. Sorry. I—uh—thought the light was nice. I can delete them if—"

"Delete them," the man repeated.

Not angry.
Not loud.
Just… absolute.

Todd swallowed and raised his camera, thumb hovering over the trash icon. He hit delete.

The man stepped closer. Close enough, Todd smelled peppermint and something metallic beneath it.

"You be careful with that thing," he said, voice low. "Some things in Pine Lakes don't like being seen."

Todd felt a cold rush along his spine.

"Right. Won't happen again."

The old man nodded once—too stiff, too precise—and returned to sweeping.

Todd backed away.

When he reached the park gate, he looked back.

The old man had stopped sweeping again.

He was watching Todd go.

A cluster of young women lounged on a blanket nearby, laughing in soft, tinkling bursts. One of them—a redhead in a sunhat large enough to double as shade for a small family—kept glancing toward Todd.

He pretended not to notice and sat on an empty bench, scrolling through his camera roll. Each photo blurred into the next—too clean, too polished, too staged.

"Hey there."

Todd looked up. And for a second, forgot how to talk.

The redhead stood before him, the sun behind her casting a soft halo around her silhouette. When she stepped closer, the light shifted to reveal delicate features, a smile that was either effortless or very practiced, and eyes the sort of blue that made people write terrible poetry.

"You must be the novelist's son," she said.

Todd squinted. "News travels fast."

"Small towns," she replied with a grin as she sat beside him. "We run on gossip and pie."

She smelled faintly of lavender. Up close, she looked almost unreal—like she belonged in one of the town's perfect window displays.

"I'm Sandra," she said. "Welcome to Pine Lakes."

"Todd." He lifted his casted arm in a half wave.

Her eyes flicked to it. "What happened?"

He deadpanned, "Mouthed off to a drug lord. He tried to cut it off. They say it's fusing back together in there."

Her expression shifted—horror, then confusion—before she caught his grin.

"Oh. You're kidding."

"Am I?" Todd grinned wider.

Sandra laughed and leaned back. "Dark humor. I like that."

"I try," he said through a bite of his sandwich.

"So, what brings you and your dad to our quiet little postcard town for book research?"

Todd shrugged. "He claims he has a story in him, but I haven't really been listening."

"Writers always have a story," she said knowingly.

"He's… between projects," Todd said. "Thought a change of scenery might help."

Sandra nodded. "This place is good for that. It keeps people… still."

Her voice lingered on the word just a second too long.

She brightened quickly. "I grew up here. My family's been in Pine Lakes since before Prohibition. I'm in medical school now—commuting about forty minutes south."

Todd raised an eyebrow. "Doctor?"

"Hematology," she said.

"Blood doctor," he replied, lifting his sandwich like a toast. "Charming."

"It's fascinating, actually. Blood tells you everything—what someone's missing, what they've endured… even what they might become."

That last word hit harder than she intended. Or maybe exactly as intended.

Changing gears, she asked, "And you? Photographer?"

Todd tapped the camera. "Freelance. Took a break after… a recent incident." He lifted the cast.

Sandra waited.

"Rehab," he admitted curtly, bracing for judgment.

But she didn't flinch—only tilted her head. "Were you serious about the drug lord?"

Todd stared at her. "I… honestly don't know anymore."

Sandra rose suddenly, brushing grass from her skirt. "There's a little gathering tonight for you and your dad. Town tradition. I'll see you there."

Before he could respond, she pulled a marker from her bag and scribbled her number across the plaster of his cast.

"Text me when you're on your way," she said, winking before she joined her friends—whose giggling sounded like rehearsed wind chimes.

Todd watched her go, smiling faintly. "That girl's gonna be the death of me," he muttered. "And I'm okay with that."

"I didn't have a party."

Todd nearly jumped off the bench.

A pale kid with messy hair sat cross-legged in the grass directly behind him, staring up with unsettling focus.

"Jesus, kid!"

"You sat next to me," the boy said matter-of-factly.

Todd blinked. "Did I? Damn."

"People don't usually notice me," the kid said. "It happens a lot."

He nodded toward Sandra. "She's totally trying to get in your pants."

Todd raised an eyebrow. "You think?"

"Oh yeah," the kid said confidently. "She wasn't lying about making newcomers feel welcome. Just… be careful."

That last part held no humor.

Todd studied him. "How old are you?"

"Fifteen and a half," the kid said instantly. "Almost sixteen. I'm Ernie."

He pointed at Todd's camera. "Is that a 5D?"

Todd hesitated, then handed it over. "Yeah."

Ernie handled it with surprising care—hands steady, practiced, reverent.

"Do you shoot manual or auto?" Ernie asked.

Todd smirked. "Manual. Always."

The kid nodded approvingly. "Good. Auto lies."

Todd blinked. Huh.

Ernie held it reverently, twisting the focus ring with precision. "You should check out the antique store. It just reopened. The old owner went and died, but the new guy's got real cameras—film, gears, the kind that smell like metal and history."

Todd's interest piqued. "That's right?"

"I can show you," Ernie said, slinging on his faded backpack. "It's not far."

Todd glanced toward the street where Sandra had disappeared, then back at Ernie.

"…Sure," he said finally, standing. "Lead the way."

Ernie grinned as if he'd just won something.

"So," Todd said, "you hang out in parks and give relationship advice to strangers?"

Ernie shrugged. "Mostly I avoid going home."

Todd raised an eyebrow. "Why?"

Ernie ignored the question. "Why are you really taking so many pictures?"

Todd hesitated. "Research. For my dad."

"Uh-huh." Ernie gave him a sideways look. "You're looking at the town like it's a puzzle."

Todd smirked. "Maybe I like puzzles."

"Good," Ernie said, kicking the pebble back toward him. "Pine Lakes is one."

They crossed the street to the doors of the antique shop tucked away in a corner, as if it were hiding secrets from the rest of the town.

Chapter Five

The Pine Lakes Public Library sat like a forgotten relic—not abandoned, just… politely ignored by time. Dust motes drifted through slanted beams of late-afternoon sunlight that filtered through stained-glass windows with the solemn hush of a church apology. Faded wallpaper peeled at the seams. The air carried the warm, papery smell of yellowed pages mixed with linseed oil.

George stepped inside and exhaled—long, steady, controlled. This was his element. Quiet places where memories hid in margins.

He approached the front desk.
The librarian—a thin woman with silver hair pinned back too tightly—didn't smile.

"Research room?" George asked.

She hesitated. "What kind of research?"

"Local history."

Another pause. Longer.
Her eyes shifted toward the back room.

"Second door on the right," she finally said. "Don't force anything open. Some cabinets stick."

George nodded, filing her unease away.

He set up at a wide oak table in the center of it all, fortified by walls of research—brittle phone books, town ledgers, microfilm printouts, newspapers browned to the color of tea. He flipped through a 1989 residential directory, fingers darkened with ink and dust. Every time he found something odd—a household that existed one year and vanished the next—he marked it with a red dot on the growing map beside him.

Thread by thread, something was taking shape.

The quiet was thick, almost sacred.

Until it wasn't.

The library's front door opened with barely a sound, but the atmosphere shifted instantly. Sunlight spilled into the dimness, and with it came someone who did not belong among dust and whispers.

Mayor Donald Merrick stepped inside.

He paused beneath the archway like some carved icon—broad shoulders, crisp shirt, posture polished to perfection. His presence hummed with charisma, a kind you felt before he even spoke. His polished shoes made no sound as he crossed the old tile floor.

George didn't look up. Not yet.

The Mayor laid a hand on his shoulder.

George jolted so violently that half his notes scattered to the floor.

"Jesus Christ!" he gasped, gripping his chest. "Don't sneak up on people in a place like this."

Donald laughed—a smooth, warm, politician's chuckle. "Didn't mean to startle you. You looked pretty locked in."

George exhaled, forcing his pulse down. "Yeah. Happens. Occupational hazard of being a writer."

Donald's eyes drifted over the chaos of the table—the notes, the red-marked maps, the missing names. "Looks like quite a project. What's the book about?"

George casually rearranged papers to hide the more damning parts. "Small-town mysteries. Thinking about a detective who retires after failing to solve a string of murders. Moves to a peaceful town. Then the killings start again. Turns out… the killer followed him."

Donald smiled faintly. "Spooky stuff."

"Small towns make the best mysteries," George said. "Everyone smiles. Everyone waves. But there's always something under the surface."

Donald leaned closer, elbows on the table. "And you think Pine Lakes fits that mold?"

George met his gaze and smiled—a practiced, unreadable smile. "It's got an atmosphere. History. The kind of place that makes a story breathe."

Donald tapped a page of red-marked names. "All these crosses and dots… looks like you're tracking something."

George shrugged. "Just population changes. Old addresses and Missing people."

He slipped his notes into his bag. "I should get back to it."

They walked toward the exit together, steps echoing softly through the cavernous room.

"You mentioned secrets and mysteries under the surface," Donald said casually.

George froze for a heartbeat—just long enough to betray the thought behind his eyes—then chuckled. "Part of the story. Fiction and reality blur when I'm in the middle of a draft."

Donald's smile widened, though his eyes didn't move. "Fiction or not, we try to keep things light around here. You can explore the darker stuff tonight."

George blinked. "Tonight?"

"Town committee's throwing a little welcome party. For you and Todd. Guests of honor."

George offered a friendly grin. "You didn't have to do that."

"It's tradition. New families deserve a warm welcome." Donald paused, lowering his voice into something teasing. "Besides, the night always ends in chaos."

George lifted an eyebrow. "Is that a promise?"

"Just Pine Lakes charm."

They parted at the steps. Donald walked toward a sleek black sedan waiting at the curb. Before getting in, he called over his shoulder:

"I was joking about the chaos."

George gave a thumbs-up.

His face said he didn't believe a word of it.

The Mayor's car pulled away from the curb.

George watched until it disappeared around the bend, then took a slow breath, letting the unease settle in his ribs like cold water. He glanced down at his ink-stained hands, at the library door behind him, at the map shoved into his bag—heavy with unanswered questions.

He needed space. Noise. Normalcy.

A place where people talked about groceries instead of whispering histories.

So, he walked.

The sun was dipping low, painting the town in warm, honeyed light as George followed the sidewalk out of the quiet historic district and into a more modern stretch of town. The storefronts grew newer. The paint brighter. The smiles practiced.

By the time he reached the Pine Lakes Shopping Center, the world had shifted from dusty stillness to evening bustle.

The Pine Lakes shopping center basked in the lazy glow of early evening. Cars crawled through the lot. A few families lingered around an ice cream stand. A woman walked a tiny dog that barked at every passing shadow.

George blended into the flow, nodding politely as he passed cheerful, too-friendly faces.

He paused outside a narrow antique shop. Through the window, Todd stood bathed in amber light, leaning over a display case of old cameras. His hand hovered above one like he feared it might vanish if he blinked.

George tapped the glass.

Todd startled, then broke into an excited grin and pointed at the camera. George stepped inside, the bell above the door chiming softly.

"Afternoon," said a slender man behind the counter. "You must be Todd's dad."

"That's me," George said, offering a handshake. "George Webb."

"Matthew Strouse," the man replied. "New to town myself." He had the polished, easy air of a man selling you something you didn't need.

George glanced around the cluttered shop—vintage clocks, tarnished silver, antiques piled like forgotten memories. "What brought you to Pine Lakes?"

"Sold my company," Matthew said with a shrug. "Took a road trip. I ended up here by accident." He smiled in a way that felt half-true. "Some places feel like they choose you, George."

George returned the smile, though his eyes scanned the man's posture, tone, hands—tiny observational habits he couldn't turn off. "I've heard that before."

Todd emerged from the back, cradling the old camera like a newborn. "This thing's a beast," he said, handing it to George. "Still works."

A wiry teenager followed behind him—messy hair, awkward posture, eager grin.

"That's Ernie," Todd said. "My unofficial tour guide."

Ernie puffed his chest a little. "I know where everything is. Even the places people don't talk about."

George raised an eyebrow. "Impressive. You sound like a man with a secret."

Ernie nodded seriously. "This town's got layers. People just don't look close enough."

George looked back at Todd. "Are you buying it?"

"Yeah," Todd said. "I want it."

Before he could pull out his wallet, Matthew waved a hand. "Take it."

George blinked. "You sure?"

"A welcome gift," Matthew said. "Every new neighbor should have one."

Todd lit up. "Thanks, man."

Ernie chimed in, "Can I get one too?"

Matthew snorted. "You steal enough already."

"Not from you," Ernie muttered.

"Still counts," Matthew shot back.

George chuckled. "There's a town party tonight. Are you going?"

Matthew gave a two-finger salute. "Wouldn't miss it."

They stepped back outside. The sunlight had softened into a golden haze. Todd examined the camera, running his fingers along the worn leather grip, the cool metal edges.

It felt real. Heavy with history.

As they walked toward the car, a sleek black sedan eased around the corner. Its tinted windows hid whoever was inside, but George recognized the car instantly.

The Mayor's.

It rolled by slowly.

Watching.

Before slipping back into traffic like a shadow.

Chapter Six

The flash of a camera lit up the party like lightning over water—brief, blinding, gone in an instant. For that heartbeat of time, everything stood still: the laughter, the splashing, the smiling faces caught mid-motion like ghosts in a photograph.

Todd weaved through the crowd, his new camera draped across his back like a sword, and his other camera in his hand. He'd been capturing everything—the barbecue smoke curling through the air, the golden shimmer of pool water, the lazy rhythm of summer bugs and classic rock. All of it seen through glass and framed in the distance.
It was easier that way. Safer to observe than to belong.

The whole party felt like a theater—faces painted in joy, gestures choreographed for the newcomer. Every laugh is a little too loud. Every wave a little too rehearsed.

He was adjusting his new camera on a tripod when a pair of soft hands slid over his shoulders. Warm. Intentional. Familiar already.

Sandra leaned in, her breath brushing his ear.
"I just ran into your dad," she whispered, her tone honeyed with mischief.
"I'm beginning to think I met the wrong Webb first."

Todd stiffened. A spark of irritation flashed behind his eyes.
"What the hell kind of thing is that to say?" he muttered, trying to keep his voice level.

Sandra circled to face him, her gaze sliding over his cameras like they were toys. "Because he's out there having a great time," she said. "And you're here pretending to be invisible."

Todd sighed, then smirked—his usual defense. He took her by the shoulders, steering her toward the tripod with his DSLR and handing her the clicker.

"Photographer, remember? You wanna help? Push that button when I say 'go.'"

He ducked behind the vintage camera. Sandra rolled her eyes but humored him.

He popped back up and humorously pointed at her. "And don't mess up. I can only do this once."

He quickly disappeared again. "Go," he called.

Click. The flash popped just as a group of teens cannonballed into the pool, water bursting into silver arcs behind them.

"Alright, help me get all this back to the Jeep," Todd said. "Then I'll let you drag me into whatever chaos you've got planned."

Sandra rolled her eyes again but clicked obediently, a crooked grin breaking through. "Deal."

Across the yard, George stood in a circle of men, hands gesturing wide as he told some story about a night in New Orleans with a crooked priest and a mistaken identity. Jack and Matthew laughed hard, slapping each other's backs, cups sloshing with cheap beer and whiskey. But George's attention wavered. His eyes flicked across the yard to Maria, who leaned against a table under a large oak, nursing a soda and watching him with that familiar, unreadable smile.

George excused himself with a nod and crossed the yard. "Thought you'd let me finish that one," he said, offering her a fresh cup.

"I was waiting to see how much of it was true," Maria said.

"Truth's flexible," he replied, smiling. "Depends on the audience."

"Is that your writer talk, or your father talk?"

He laughed softly. "Maybe both."

She held his gaze. "You were the kind of kid who told stories no one believed, weren't you?"

"Yeah," he admitted. "But they listened anyway."

Maria took a sip. "People remember good stories more than they remember facts."

He nodded, the laughter around them fading for a moment. "You get it."

A flash cut across their faces—camera light. They turned to see Todd taking a photo of Sandra. She posed with random people as they walked to the Jeep.

"He makes friends fast," Maria said.

George smiled faintly. "He had to. We moved a lot when he was younger. He learned to read people. Give them what they need."

"That's not learning to connect," she said softly. "That's learning to survive."

George looked away, expression tightening. "Same thing sometimes."

Two heavy hands landed on his shoulders.

"Beautiful, isn't it?"

George turned. The Mayor stood there in his pressed linen suit, drink in hand, grinning like a man carved from charm itself.

"The party?" George asked, still shaking off the sudden touch.

Donald shook his head slowly, like a preacher mid-sermon. "The community. The connection. All these people are coming together to welcome you. That's what the world needs more of."

George smiled politely. "You're not wrong. You've got something special here."

Donald nodded. "Belonging doesn't just happen. You have to shape it. Help people find where they fit."

Maria's polite smile didn't reach her eyes.

"Are you planning on sticking around?" Donald asked, his voice smooth as silk.

"Once the book's done, maybe," George said. "Maybe I'm ready to stop drifting."

Donald raised his cup. "To finding home."

He kissed Maria's hand lightly, winked, and drifted back into the sea of laughter and light—vanishing as if he'd never been there.

As the night deepened, the party spilled down to the dock, where tiki torches lined a narrow path to a houseboat glowing with music and movement—strings of lights glittered on the water, reflections trembling with every ripple.

"Come on, new guy!" someone shouted from the deck.

Sandra pulled Todd's hand as they trotted down the dock. "Are you hesitating?"

Todd eyed the swaying boat. "Is this your idea of fun?"

"We live in the middle of nowhere," she said. "You make your own fun."

He smirked. "Are there gonna be drugs?"

Sandra flashed a devilish grin and opened the gate. "Only the best."

The air was thick with sweat, perfume, and something sweetly chemical—almost metallic. The music swallowed them as they stepped aboard—bass thumping through the boards, laughter spilling like smoke. Bodies moved in a slow, dizzy rhythm, sharing bottles and touches as if everything belonged to everyone.

Ernie appeared like a trick of light—ghosting through the crowd, pocketing wallets and drinks with practiced ease. He flashed Todd a grin—too wide, too knowing—and disappeared below deck.

Sandra led Todd down a narrow stairwell, into a small bedroom bathed in red light. She pressed him back onto the bed and climbed over him, eyes half-shadowed, half-burning.
From the nightstand, she drew a small amber vial.

"Open," she whispered.

He obeyed.

The liquid hit his tongue—sweet, then metallic and his head began to spin.

"What was that?" he asked, voice thick.

Sandra smiled. "Do you really care?"

No. He didn't.

The room tilted gently, the red lights pulsing in slow, viscous waves. Todd blinked hard, trying to anchor himself, but the world had gone soft at the edges.

When he sat up, Sandra was already gone.

The door to the cabin stood open, music leaking through it in thick vibrations. Todd steadied himself on the wall and stepped into the narrow hallway. The floor swayed under him, the boat shifting with the lake.

He drifted toward the sound.

The lights were dimmer now—colorless, humming faintly. Bodies moved in slow motion, their silhouettes bending and twisting. Two men stood near the bar, gripping the same bottle. Todd frowned as one leaned in—mouth open wider than seemed normal—pressing his face toward the other's neck.

For a moment, he swore he saw teeth. But then someone walked between them, and the image broke like a bubble.

A woman sat in a corner booth, head tilted back, laughing silently while another girl leaned over her. The girl's hair fell like a curtain, hiding whatever she was doing.

Todd raised his camera on instinct.

Click.

The flash strobed the booth.

For one frame—just one—he thought he saw the girl's eyes flare white and reflective, like an animal caught in headlights.

He pushed through a cluster of dancing bodies. Their movements felt synchronized as though they were following a single invisible rhythm. Hands grazing him as he passed.

Todd made his way toward the deck, desperate for air.

Outside, the night felt alive. The lake breathed mist across the railing, curling around his arms like grasping fingers. A couple stood against the far rail, whispering. The woman ran her hand down the man's throat, then pressed her lips to his neck—

Todd looked away and moved down a narrow walkway toward the bow, where a man stood alone, silhouetted by moonlight. His posture was still—unnaturally so.

He backed up until his shoulder hit the doorframe. The music pulsed like a heartbeat. Shadows stretched along the deck, reaching for his feet, his legs.

He blinked, and they disappeared.

Someone shouted his name from inside.

But the voice… didn't sound like Sandra.

Todd turned, unsteady, and saw a shape slipping through the doorway—lean, tall, limbs too long.

He bolted toward the exit ladder and climbed down to dry land, or at least closer to it. He stumbled down the dock, shirt clinging to him, eyes glassy, lips tingling with that faint metallic taste. The night hummed with insects and distant laughter. The torches burned low, flickering like dying stars.

He wandered through the silent streets of Pine Lakes, camera hanging loosely from his neck. Porch lights glowed like guardian eyes as crickets chirped a soothing song.

He reached a cul-de-sac and stopped. The moon hung enormous and pale above the rooftops, washing everything in cold silver.

Todd raised the camera. Click.

The shutter snapped—and something answered.

A howl. Low and mournful.

Then another—closer. Sharper.

A crash echoed down the block. Something heavy hit metal.

Todd turned, heart hammering, breath fogging the cool air. The house beside him stood dark and still.

But something moved.

Something was there.

And still, he walked toward it.

Chapter Seven

The porch light flicked on with a faint hum.

A bloodied hand slammed against the glass from inside the house.

Todd froze in the yard, breath catching mid-step. For a heartbeat, he couldn't move—just stood there, adrenaline flooding his veins as crimson fingers trembled against the window. Whatever horror lurked behind the pane stayed hidden in shadow.

Then—

CRASH.

A metallic bang thundered from the back of the house—louder, deeper—like a door being ripped from its hinges.

Todd snapped out of it and ran.

He darted down the side yard, weeds slapping his jeans. The porch light's glow barely reached the fence line; everything beyond was swallowed by darkness. Every crunch of his shoes on gravel felt deafening.

He rounded the corner—

and stopped cold.

The back door hung by a single hinge, splintered and half-torn away. Wood shards and metal screws littered the steps, as if something enormous had erupted from inside.

Todd crept forward, pulse pounding in his ears. He hesitated at the threshold, then stepped into the house.

The kitchen was hell.

The walls bore the frenzied brushstrokes of violence. Blood painted the walls and ceiling in wide, chaotic streaks, still slick and dark. The refrigerator, the counters, the broken table, all smeared with red. Dishes were shattered across the floor. A chair lay snapped in half near the sink.

And in the middle of it all, sprawled like a puppet with its strings cut, was Matthew.

Or what was left of him.

His body was shredded open. Rib bones jutted through the meat. One arm was gone below the elbow. His face was barely recognizable, jaw slack, eyes wide. Whatever had killed him hadn't just attacked—it had fed.

Blood pooled thick around the corpse, seeping into the tile. A long, sticky smear led from the body out through the doorway—something had dragged most of Matthew away.

Todd staggered back, bile climbing his throat. He pressed against the doorframe and raised his camera, his hands shaking. The shutter clicked once—loud as a gunshot in the silence. Then again.
And again.

He had to document it. Proof meant control.

Then—
a howl.

Low. Hungry. Inhuman.

Todd's head snapped up.

He flicked on his phone's flashlight. The beam quivered across the grass, tracing the smear of blood toward the woods. The air grew colder with each step he took. Fog rolled low across the ground, thick and fast, curling around his ankles like smoke.

He hesitated.

Then stepped into the trees.

The canopy above swallowed the light. Branches arched overhead like a cage. The trail of blood thinned, then vanished, lost in the swirling mist. Todd spun in a slow circle, trying to retrace his steps—but everything looked the same. The fog distorted distance; direction slipped away.

Snap.

A twig behind him.

He spun, flashlight up. Nothing. Just white mist and dark trunks. His foot caught on a root, and before he could catch himself—

Crash.

He hit the ground hard, pain screaming up his leg.

"Ah—come on—"

He grabbed his shin. Blood soaked through torn denim, gleaming in the flashlight beam. Beneath him jutted a rusted water pipe—broken, jagged.

"Shit…"

He pulled himself forward, dragging inch by inch through the mud. The fog pressed in tighter, muffling the world until only his breath and heartbeat remained.

His hand struck wood.

A tall privacy fence loomed ahead. Behind it, a house silhouette glowed faintly yellow from an upstairs window. Todd crawled along the fence until he found a narrow gate and shoved through.

The yard beyond was unnaturally still. Not just empty—untouched. No grass clippings, no footprints, no sign of life. Just an old, rusted AC unit and the steady hum of electricity. One window burned with a soft amber light.

He limped toward it, every step a jolt of pain. He climbed onto the rusty unit and lifted his camera toward the window.

And froze.

The Mayor.

Naked, standing in the middle of a steamed-up bathroom, his body bathed in soft light. But it wasn't his nakedness that froze Todd. It was the carvings. His chest, back, and thighs were etched with patterns and symbols. Some looked like constellations, others like symbols of power and sacrifice. Some scabbed over. Others still raw. It looked like a language or old ritualistic markings.

Donald stared into the mirror with eerie calm, his fingertips brushing each mark like a man in prayer. Then, wordlessly, he stepped into the shower and began to rinse the blood from his body.

Todd raised his camera.
Click.

The sound was faint, he leaned in for another angle—but the AC unit shifted under his weight. The rusted metal bent, groaned—then collapsed.

Then—SNAP.

The whole thing collapsed.

Todd hit the ground hard, stifling a cry. He rolled behind the unit, clutching the camera tight. His heart was hammering in his throat.

The water inside stopped, and the window above creaked open.

Then—footsteps. Wet. Deliberate.

The back door eased open.

Donald stepped outside.
Barefoot. Shirtless. Steam rising from his skin. His head tilted, nostrils flaring, not just sniffing, but inhaling the air like a man who knew the smell of fear and blood.

His gaze swept the yard, slowly, then stopped.

Todd froze, not even breathing.

Donald cocked his head, listening…

Then turned, calm as ever, and walked back inside.

The door closed with a soft click.

Todd stayed motionless, the cold seeping into his bones. His leg throbbed. His camera was safely in his hand. He breathed, shallow and silent, until exhaustion took him and the night swallowed everything.

The world shifted around him.

Dreams bled into darkness. Darkness bled into pale gray.

Sound returned first—distant birdsong. Then the soft hiss of sprinklers. Then warmth.

He woke to light.

The morning sun cut through the fog, pale and clean. Dew beaded the grass. Birds chirped faintly. The world looked surgically repaired.

He sat up slowly. The Mayor's house loomed behind him—quiet, undisturbed.

"Son of a bitch," he muttered.

No sirens. No signs of struggle. Nothing.

He checked his camera. Working.

His phone. Still on with more missed phone calls from his father than he could count. He limped through the gate and back onto the street. The town was waking up—porch lights clicking off, sprinklers hissing, as if the night had never happened.

He turned down his block.

George and Maria sat on the porch, coffee in hand. They both stood as he approached.

"What the hell happened to you?" George said.

Maria's eyes widened. "Todd—are you okay?"

Todd stopped at the steps. Blood. Mud. Bruises. He looked wrecked. But alive.

"I was taking pictures," he said. "Saw that wolf again. Fell. Must've blacked out."

"A wolf?" Maria echoed.

George nodded. "He said one attacked him a few nights ago."

Maria frowned. "Why didn't you tell me?"

George shrugged. "We live in the middle of nowhere. Figured it wasn't a big deal."

"Wolves don't usually attack people," Maria said quietly.

Her gaze dropped to his leg. "You're bleeding."

"I've had worse," Todd muttered, forcing a half-smile and lifting his arm as he brushed past them into the house.

Maria turned to George. "Did he really see a wolf?"

George took a long sip of coffee, watching the street. "He saw something."

Maria crossed her arms. "I'm reporting it. Better safe than sorry."

George nodded slowly.
But his eyes had changed.

Todd was covered in mud and blood, telling a wild story that mirrored his worst mistakes back home.

George wasn't sure what his son had seen, only that he was starting to lose his trust again.

Chapter Eight

The doorbell rang just as sunlight began to crawl across the warped hardwood of Todd's bedroom floor, splashing pale light onto his cluttered room. It dragged him from the depths of a dreamless, heavy sleep, his body aching with the memory of what had happened the night before. Each limb screamed protest as he sat up, his muscles stiff, joints swollen, and the dried sting of old blood flaring alive again.

Another knock.

The knock came again. He rubbed his eyes with the back of his hand and stumbled down the hallway, still wearing the same torn jeans and a shirt smeared with pine needles and crusted sweat.

When he opened the door, the morning light hit him full in the face.

Sandra stood there. Her hair was pulled back beneath a ball cap, and she wore an oversized flannel like armor. Her eyes darted immediately to the cuts on his arm, narrowing with concern as they took in the jagged gash just under the rolled sleeve.

"Oh my God," she whispered. "Maria said you came home looking like you'd been hit by a truck."

Todd scratched at his temple, squinting through the haze. "Took a wrong turn," he mumbled. "Fell down a hill."

Sandra didn't buy it. She stepped closer, fingertips brushing one of the deeper wounds. Todd flinched.

"I knew I shouldn't have let you off that damn boat," she said, voice almost joking—but layered under the humor was something heavier.

He caught her hand and moved it gently away. "I'll live. Just stop poking my holes."

Sandra smiled, though her eyes lingered on the bruises. "You sure?"

"Mostly."

A beat of silence hung between them.

"I'm heading to lunch soon," she said finally. "That diner with the terrible fries. You in?"

Todd hesitated in the doorway, fighting the fog in his head. "Yeah... just let me clean up first."

"I'll see you soon," she said, stepping off the porch. "Don't ghost me."

He watched her walk away, then closed the door and leaned against it, exhaling. His ribs throbbed with every breath. His brain felt submerged — too much noise, too little clarity.

From another room, footsteps.

"Who was that?" George asked, walking in, beard damp from a rinse, buttoning his shirt.

"Sandra," Todd said. "Wants to grab lunch."

George gave a knowing grin. "Nice. Speaking of lunch, the Mayor called. Invited me over."

Todd froze mid-step. "Why?"

"No idea," George said. "But I'm not about to pass up a meeting with Pine Lakes' puppet master. The more he talks, the more he slips."

Todd pulled a clean shirt from a chair, wincing as he slid it over his shoulder. "You gonna tell him what I saw?"

George looked up sharply. "Maybe. Depends."

Todd froze, eyes locking with his father's. "Don't. Not yet."

George's brow furrowed. "Why not?"

"Because…" Todd hesitated, struggling to articulate the fear tightening in his chest. "I don't think it's the right time."

George studied him for a long moment. Then he nodded. "Alright. But we can't stay quiet forever. You keep showing up covered in blood, and people will start to question things."

George clapped his shoulder and left. Todd hobbled through the house and into his room. He lingered at the edge, staring at the half-played Risk board on the dresser. He sat, reached for a pipe — then stopped.

Instead, he grabbed the bong from the windowsill, packed it, and lit it. The smoke curled upward, slow and lazy, clouding the light.

Through the haze, his reflection in the window stared back — eyes dark, rimmed with exhaustion.

And then he saw the camera.

He picked it up and flipped through the photos.

There it was.

Matthew.

Twisted, bloodied, half-eaten on the kitchen floor.

Todd's chest tightened. He swallowed hard, checked the time, and headed out.

The neighborhood looked ordinary. Birds chirped. A lawnmower buzzed somewhere down the street.

Todd stood across the street from Matthew's house, frozen. In daylight, the place looked... normal. Peaceful, even. No police tape. No ambulances. No crowd. No sign that anything horrific had ever happened.

He crossed the street slowly, camera in hand.

He snapped a photo of the front window—the same window that had been smeared with blood. Now spotless.

He walked the path around back, heart hammering louder with each step.

The kitchen door had been blown off its hinges the night before. Now it hung neatly on its frame, perfectly intact.

He raised the camera again, adjusting the lens.

Then — a creak.

The back door opened.

Todd froze.

And out stepped Matthew.

Alive. Whole. A little pale, but healthier than he'd ever looked.

"Hey, man," Matthew said cheerfully. "What's up?"

Todd's breath caught. "You're… okay?"

Matthew tilted his head. "Yeah? You good?"

Todd forced a shaky grin. "Just… taking pictures for the book."

Matthew laughed. "Oh, right! Hey, did you get that old one working?"

"Sure did," Todd said, words thick on his tongue.

"Cool. Bring the shots when they're developed."

Todd nodded numbly. "Yeah. I will."

He turned and walked away before his mind could catch up — before reality could unravel.

Todd didn't slow down until he reached the end of the block. His pulse refused to settle, the world feeling two steps out of sync. Matthew's cheerful wave replayed in his mind like a glitching tape.

He needed air. He needed normalcy. He needed… something to anchor him.

Lunch.

Sandra.

Right.

He rechecked the time, wiped his palms on his jeans, and forced his breathing to steady as he headed toward town.

By the time he reached the diner, the world had snapped back into its bright, ordinary shape.

The diner buzzed with chatter when Todd arrived. Sandra sat with a few of the kids from the party — laughing, nursing hangovers, filling the booth with noise and grease.

Todd slid into the booth across from her.

"Didn't know it was a group hang," he said.

"Didn't know you'd actually show," Sandra shot back.

"That would've been rude," he said, trying to keep the mood light. He tapped his cast against the table. "And I'm not rude. Not anymore."

The bell above the door chimed.

Ernie strolled in, grinning. One of the guys shouted, "Ernie! You stole beer off my boat!"

Ernie cackled. "You shouldn't leave good beer out in the open."

He dragged over a chair, flopped down, and looked Todd up and down. "Jesus. You look like you lost a fight with a bear."

"Wolf," Todd said.

The laughter died instantly.

Forks hovered in midair. The waitress froze behind the counter. Even the kitchen went silent.

Todd blinked, glancing around. "What?"

Ernie cleared his throat. "Never seen a wolf around here. Probably a coyote. Or maybe you were wasted."

Gradually, sound returned — clattering dishes, murmured voices.

Todd leaned toward Sandra. "What the hell was that?"

She didn't answer. Her fingers tapped nervously against her glass. Her eyes flicked toward the kitchen.

"This town's weird," Todd muttered. "Like something out of an '80s sitcom."

"The kind where the neighbors vanish, and nobody notices?" Sandra said.

"The kind where the dead come back to life twenty minutes after they were murdered," Todd said, the words barely a whisper. "Exactly."

"You'd be surprised what people can ignore," Ernie muttered.

"You couldn't get away with that now," Todd said, almost to himself.

"Oh, you'd be surprised, it still happens all the time. The human race has just gotten dumber," Ernie muttered.

The bell over the door rang again.

Todd turned.

Matthew.

Picking up takeout and waving to the waitress like nothing was wrong.

Todd's blood went cold.

He stood abruptly.

"Hey," Sandra said. "You just got here."

"I know. I have to go." He spoke as he walked away

Sandra threw her hands on the table in frustration. "What happened to not being rude?"

Todd walked out the door. "I'll make it up to you," he said, looking back one last time.

Ernie leaned back. "I'll find you tonight," he called. "We'll hunt your ghost wolf."

But Todd didn't answer.

He was already gone, pulse pounding, the world tilting beneath him.

Something was wrong with Pine Lakes.
And Matthew was only the beginning.

Chapter Nine

Todd stepped out of the sandwich shop just in time to catch a glimpse of Matthew disappearing around the corner. He wasn't sure why he noticed—just a flicker of movement, a familiar stride, the same blue shirt he'd seen that morning. Something about it set off an instinct, a tug in his gut that told him to move.

He shoved the half-eaten sandwich into the trash and followed, keeping low and quiet. His boots thudded on the sidewalk until he veered off into the dirt path that wound behind the row of storefronts. The town was eerily calm for midday—no cars, no chatter, just the whisper of trees swaying slightly in the wind. Even the birds seemed to know better than to make noise here.

As he rounded the corner, he spotted Matthew again—this time paused at the intersection across from the church. Sunlight spilled over the roof and the steeple like a silent blessing, but Todd felt nothing sacred about it. He ducked into a cluster of overgrown trees near the sidewalk and knelt behind a utility box, pulling his camera from his backpack with slow, measured movements.

Through the viewfinder, he saw Matthew check his phone. Then, from the opposite side of the street, came the Mayor and, to Todd's disbelief, his father.

They met like old friends. Laughing. Shaking hands.

Todd's stomach turned.

Donald clapped Matthew on the shoulder. George returned it with a nod, all smiles—the perfect southern charm. Todd pressed the shutter halfway down and began snapping in bursts, thumb cushioning the sound of each click.

"George, this is Matthew Strouse," the Mayor said. "He moved here a few months back."

George chuckled. "Yeah, we met at his shop yesterday. Thanks again for the camera."

"No problem at all," Matthew said. "I actually just ran into Todd—he was in my backyard taking photos."

George's smile turned brittle. "I hope he didn't bother you. He's just trying to get a layout. A book's only as good as its details."

Matthew shrugged with a polite chuckle. "No bother at all. I've never met a writer before."

Before the conversation could go any further, the Mayor took a step forward and clapped his hands.

"Well, George, lunch was fantastic. But Matthew has volunteered to run the AV department in the church once the renovations are complete. I'm going to show him what he'll be working with."

"Still on for golf tomorrow?" George asked.

Donald nodded with a grin. "Wouldn't miss it. I gotta work on my backswing."

Todd's camera clicked once more, capturing the handshake and parting smiles. As George turned back toward the house, Donald and Matthew headed up the path to the church.

Todd slipped from behind the trees and crossed the street silently, sticking close to the hedges along the sidewalk. He reached the side of the church just in time to see them step through the wide double doors. He jogged to the rear of the building and peeked into a window covered mostly by plastic sheeting. He shifted to another—this one uncovered—and caught a glimpse inside.

Matthew and the Mayor stood before a pair of old wooden doors at the base of the sanctuary, doors Todd hadn't noticed before. They opened them with effort, revealing a stairwell that plunged into darkness.

They began their descent.

Click.

Todd captured the shot. He zoomed in, steadying his breath, then ducked down and reviewed the photo. It was clear enough—grainy but unmistakable. Donald and Matthew descended into what looked like a cellar beneath the church.

The camera trembled slightly in his hands. His stomach churned—not from fear, but from validation. This was real. It was happening. And George had no clue.

Todd backed away from the church, careful not to crack a twig or rustle a leaf. The whole town felt like it was listening. Watching. Waiting for him to slip.

He walked the long way home, sticking to alleys and side streets, checking over his shoulder every few steps.
Every window felt like an eye.
Every shadow felt like a mouth.

By the time he reached his street, the daylight had thinned into evening. Porch lights flicked on one by one as if the houses were preparing for something he couldn't name.

Todd trudged up the cracked driveway, exhausted, when the front door slammed open.

George stood there, red-faced and angry.

"Hey, asshole," he called out.

Todd froze. "What?"

"I told you, Todd. Why the hell are you taking pictures of people's houses?"

Todd walked past him without answering, his shoulders stiff.

George followed. "I'm talking to you!"

Todd spun at the porch steps. "I'm working on a theory. About the case. You know—the case you're supposed to be working on!"

George's face twisted in confusion and frustration.

Todd kept going. "We've been here three days, and you've already bought in. Playing golf, doing lunches. You're socializing, Dad. You're losing the edge. This isn't even my investigation, and I've put in more time than you. You want to ride my ass about being serious? Look in the mirror."

"I am working on it," George said, jaw clenched.

"One study session at the library doesn't count."

Todd pushed through the front door. George followed him into the hallway.

"I'm accessing the historic records," George argued. "From there, I can get housing data, utilities, and migration history. I can prove who lived here and who didn't. You need to trust me."

Todd whirled around. "Trust you? You're the one rubbing elbows with the guy who might be behind the entire conspiracy."

"Jesus, Todd—who are you even talking about now?"

"Matthew. Donald. Take your pick. You want to talk about getting us in trouble? How about the guy who invited a total stranger into the church basement like it was a clubhouse?"

George's eyes narrowed. "What do you mean, the basement?"

Todd stormed into his room and pulled a photo from a pile on his desk. He shoved it toward his father. "Here. Last night. I followed a blood trail to a house. Thought it was abandoned. Wasn't. It was his. The Mayor's."

George stared at the image—Matthew's limp body sprawled across a blood-slick kitchen floor.

"What is this?" he asked, voice barely a whisper.

"I told you. Blood. Tattoos. Rituals. The guy was covered in markings. And I followed the trail straight into that house."

"That's ridiculous," George said, laughing nervously. "You think the Mayor is murdering people in his basement? You sound like a lunatic."

Todd snapped. "You know what's ridiculous? You see me as a screw-up every time I open my mouth. You brought me here. I'm a journalist just like you. But all you see is the addict."

George looked like he was about to say something—but instead, his fist flew.

It connected with Todd's jaw with a loud crack, sending him sprawling across the room.

There was a stunned silence.

Todd sat up slowly, holding his mouth. "You hit me," he said softly. "You actually hit me."

George stood over him, breathing hard.

"I brought you here to keep you out of jail," he said coldly. "You want to help? Find the wolf. Real evidence. Not this blurry bullshit."

He grabbed the photo from the floor and held it up. "This isn't evidence. It's a joke. Looks like you tried to get an upskirt photo of some chick at a party. It's trash."

George threw the photo onto the Risk board on the table, scattering plastic soldiers and countries across the floor. He stormed out, the front door slamming behind him.

Todd stayed where he was, gathering the game pieces slowly. He picked up the photo last, holding it in the light. It was blurry. The focus was off. The framing is bad. But the blood was there. The shape on the floor—human. The Mayor'swallpaper is visible in the background.

It wasn't enough. But it was real.

George threw on his jacket and stormed out of the house. As his hand met the handle, there was a knock. He slowly opened it to see Ernie standing there, slightly out of breath.

George didn't react; he just moved past him like he didn't exist.

"Ernie's the name, sir," he said. "Is Todd around?"

From behind, George shouted without turning. "Let yourself in. He's in his room."

Then the sound of retreating footsteps and the creak of the gate as George disappeared across the yard.

Chapter Ten

Todd sat in his dimly lit room, walls swallowed by a chaotic collage of photographs.

Grainy zooms of distant faces. Houses frozen at dusk. The edge of shadows. Flickers of movement in treetops.

Each picture was another piece of the puzzle, only he cared enough to assemble—connected by red yarn, frantic notes, and questions the town preferred to bury. A police blotter from 2003. A newspaper clipping about a boating accident. A faded group photo outside the church, half the faces circled in Sharpie.

His cheek still throbbed from the punch his father had thrown earlier—a deep, pulsing ache that grounded him more than it hurt.

But it wasn't the bruise that bothered him. It was the look.

That split second where his father hadn't recognized him—hadn't seen Todd the way a father is supposed to see a son.

Just a threat.

Just a liability.

Just another problem.

He felt it gnawing at him now, sitting in the blue glow of the monitor: maybe George didn't want the truth. Maybe he couldn't handle it. Maybe no one in this town wanted it.

He stepped back and pinned up two new photos:

Matthew slipping into the church beside the Mayor.

And George, lingering at the gate, unaware that Todd had been watching.

A floorboard creaked behind him.

Ernie stepped inside. His eyes drifted across the wall, shifting from confusion… to amusement… to something like unease.

"Jesus, man," he murmured.

Todd didn't turn. He shoved a stack of boxes aside. A dozen GoPros spilled across the floor, clattering loudly. Ernie jumped back.

"I like what you've got going on," Ernie said, crouching beside him. "But what the hell is all this?"

Todd didn't answer. He swept the cameras quickly into a backpack, movements efficient, practiced. The intensity of the hunt felt familiar, a cold, focused rush that had replaced every other compulsion. The obsession had eaten him from the inside out, but it also made him razor-focused.

"Where'd you come from?" Todd finally asked.

"Front door. Your dad let me in. He looked pissed."

Todd gave a vague nod and slung the backpack over his shoulder. "He always is. Stay here. I'll be back in an hour."

He grabbed his hoodie and camera, pausing in the doorway.

"Don't touch anything."

He meant it.

Outside, the sky sagged under heavy clouds. Todd crouched on the porch, dug through his bag, and pulled out a GoPro and a roll of duct tape. The camera blinked to life with a soft red glow. He taped it to the corner beam, angling it at the front door.

A silent alarm. A watcher for the watchers.

Then he moved into the street. Step by step. Camera by camera. Shadow to shadow.

Like the whole town was breathing around him.

At one house, a curtain snapped shut the moment his foot touched their lawn.

At the corner, a sprinkler stopped mid-cycle as if someone had turned it off to listen.

Todd planted a camera in a mailbox—another under a lamppost and another in the low branches of a pine tree overlooking the church.

The church loomed like a dark spine in the distance, its windows reflecting nothing. As he crossed the final street, he caught movement in an upstairs window.

A face.

Pale and still.

Watching him.

Not blinking.

He froze.

The face didn't move.

Didn't tilt.

Just stared.

Todd backed away slowly, pretending to be checking his phone, pretending he hadn't seen anything wrong.

"Okay," he whispered. "Okay. That's new."

He stayed hidden until the quiet returned—until the world exhaled again—before making his way back home.

Inside, the computers hummed as they powered on. Ernie drifted toward them, curiosity eating away at any hesitation. The monitors lit up one by one—feeds from all over Pine Lakes. Their street. The alley behind the house. The treeline near the forest. A shaky, zoomed-in angle fixed on the church doors.

"Whoa…" Ernie whispered, leaning closer.

His gaze flicked to the bong on the desk. Temptation did the rest. He packed a bowl, sparked it, and leaned back into the blue glow of the screens.

Hours bled by quietly.
Some feeds were frozen.
Others hissed with static.
The rest showed unsettling stillness—vacant streets, blank windows, shadows that felt like they were breathing.

Hours later, Todd showed back up on his front steps after completing his mission. The front door opened softly. Todd trudged in, exhausted, and collapsed into his chair. He grabbed a cold beer can from the cooler beside the desk and pressed it against his bruised cheek, eyes heavy.

Then—pssshhk.

A second can hissed behind him, spraying a thin mist across his neck.

Todd sat upright instantly. Confusion froze into terror.

The Mayor stood in the middle of the room.

He didn't belong there—yet somehow looked perfectly at home. One hand held a beer. The other dangled at his side. His expression wasn't angry. If anything, he looked… curious. Pleased, even.

"Todd," he said softly. "You've been busy."

Todd couldn't move. His breath felt stuck in his chest.

The Mayor walked to the window, peering out into the quiet street. His movements were slow, precise—an unsettling grace to them.

"Cameras on the porch," he murmured. "Some in the trees. One in the church. You've been documenting people."

Todd swallowed hard. "Maria asked me to help. She wanted footage of… the thing I saw."

The Mayor tilted his head slightly, the faintest smile tugging at his lip. "Did she now?"

His tone wasn't accusing. It was worse—like he was weighing how much of Todd's statement was fear… and how much was truth.

"What did this thing look like?" he asked and drained the rest of his beer.

Todd hesitated. "Big. Black. Mangy. Huge teeth."

The Mayor crushed the can in one hand—easily—and tossed it across the room into the trash. The clang echoed like a warning.

"And you saw it?"

Todd nodded. "A few nights ago. And again last night."

A dry laugh scraped out of the Mayor. "Kid, this is the middle of nowhere. Animals roam free. You'd do well to remember that."

Todd's voice dropped. "But what if it's dangerous?"

"Oh, it is dangerous," the Mayor said, voice sharpening to a quiet blade. "Everything is. This land—this town—it was built on old foundations. People came here to escape the world, not rebuild it."

He turned from the window. His eyes caught the monitor light, glowing strangely.

"You and your father are guests here. Don't forget that. I know your past—and your failures. This town doesn't need your baggage."

Silence thickened the air. Todd's heartbeat thundered.

The Mayor stepped closer—not threateningly, not loudly, just… inevitably. He leaned in until their faces were inches apart.

"Take the cameras down."

It wasn't a request.

He turned back to the window, expression unreadable.

Ernie stirred on the bed, eyes half-lidded. "Todd?" he mumbled.

Todd flinched—and when he glanced back toward the Mayor…

He was gone.

Vanished.

No footsteps.

No shift in air.

No sound.

Todd scrambled to the window, scanning the yard, the street, the shadows between houses.

Nothing.

Ernie rubbed his face. "Who were you talking to?"

Todd didn't answer.

He just stared out into the quiet dark—watching, waiting—for the thing that might still be out there.

The thing that might already be inside.

Chapter Eleven

George sat silently in the wooden chair, a towel draped loosely over his shoulders, his bare chest catching the chill of the night air. The faint scent of lake water mixed with pine drifted through the open window, where the moon hung low and full above the glassy surface of the lake. Its reflection rippled softly, distorted by the quiet movement of the water — a false twin shimmering in unrest. George's eyes were locked on it, unmoving, as if hypnotized.

Behind him, Maria moved like fog — silent and slow. She emerged from the darkness, barefoot, a silk robe barely tied to the waist. Her presence filled the room like perfume: subtle, lingering, inescapable. She knelt behind him, her hands sliding down his chest — cold at first, then warm as his skin adjusted. Her fingers traced the stress written in his muscles, memorizing the tension.

"So tense," she whispered, her voice delicate and tender. "You hold it all here. Right behind your heart."

George didn't flinch, but a sigh escaped him. "Todd…" His voice cracked slightly, and he exhaled again, heavier. "I always had such high hopes for him. We gave him everything. A stable home. The best schools. Opportunities I never had growing up."

His gaze didn't leave the lake.

"And for a while, it looked like it was working. He was thriving — college honors, that big internship lined up. Hell, I thought he was going to do something meaningful. Something clean." George's fingers tapped the towel draped across his lap, restless. "But one bad night. Just one. And it all unraveled."

Maria listened, her fingers slowing. She leaned in, her lips grazing his ear. "The world has a way of unraveling even the best of plans," she said.

"I sold the old house. Cashed out retirement accounts. Pulled favors to keep his record sealed. Paid for the best rehab money could buy. And still… he's here causing trouble where it's not needed."

Maria turned his face toward her — gentle but firm. "You think he's failing you again?"

"I think… I'm tired of carrying him," George said, the words coming out hollow. "And I'm scared of what's going to happen."

Maria kissed his temple. "Then stop carrying him. Let him fall. Some people have to break before they know how to stand."

George's eyes flicked to hers — the flicker of guilt behind them, briefly extinguished by the strange calm in her gaze. Calm, and something darker. Something that whispered: you already know he won't get back up.

"You're quite the convincing lady," he murmured.

She smiled, slow and seductive. "Now come to bed."

George rose, sweeping her into his arms. The shadows of the bedroom swallowed them as the lake outside stilled once more, the moonlight stretching like a silver blade across the water.

While George let himself be pulled deeper into the quiet seduction of the night, another room in Pine Lakes was lit by a very different kind of intimacy—the glow of monitors, the hum of paranoia, and the frantic energy of a young man who could no longer sleep.

Todd sat hunched in his computer chair, eyes bloodshot and wired, locked on the sprawl of photographs and notes taped across his wall. Newspaper clippings, blurry party snapshots, candid shots of townsfolk walking, standing, laughing. He traced one line with his finger — a red string connecting a picture of the Mayor at the pool party to a yellowing article about the town's founding families.

He paused at a picture of the church. "You're hiding something under there," he muttered.

The desk beside him was littered with half-empty Red Bulls, open notebooks, and crumpled candy wrappers. His laptop was running, displaying real-time camera feeds from around town. Most were empty, except for the occasional flicker of motion — a shadow, a figure passing too quickly across the frame.

From the bed, Ernie stirred, scratching his face and taking a slow sip of beer. "Are you talking to the wall again?"

Todd barely turned. "Have you ever worked in a darkroom?"

Ernie blinked. "Like… a developing room? Or like a panic room?"

"I need to process film. Some ancient film," Todd said, standing suddenly. "All the digital stuff is glitching. Something's off. But I want to see what's on that old slate."

Ernie groaned as he stood. "Alright, Spielberg. Let's build you a murder lab."

The basement was transformed by necessity and caffeine. The two of them worked like men possessed — Todd clearing space, Ernie cutting black plastic garbage bags to line the walls, duct tape hissing with each pull, covering every seam. The single bulb overhead flickered before Todd replaced it with a red light. The room turned dark, surreal — like blood underwater.

Todd moved carefully, fingers trembling with exhaustion as he guided the negatives through the chemical baths. Developer. Stop. Fixer. He hung the prints on a clothesline, watching as faces began to emerge like ghosts out of the mist.

One by one, the town's secrets materialized.

Faces slowly emerged on the hanging prints—some familiar, some distorted, some wrong.
Todd stared at them too long, long enough for the edges of his vision to blur. The red light buzzed. His head drooped. Darkness took him.

He woke with a jolt, head resting on a pile of old rags, the chemical tang of fixer still in the air. The red bulb buzzed faintly overhead. He checked his phone: 11:30 a.m., and there were missed calls from his father.

Ernie was gone.

Todd stood, joints stiff, and turned to the drying prints.

His stomach dropped.

In the photo, a large group that had once filled the frame was gone. Not blurred. Not hidden.
Gone.

He flipped back and forth between frames. In one, the pool party was packed — teenagers diving, George manning the grill, Donald sipping wine.

In the newer print, Donald was missing. Just… not there.

A cold wave washed over Todd. He grabbed the rest of the photos and sprinted upstairs.

At the coffee table, Todd spread out every photo he had. On the left: prints from his digital camera. On the right: the developed plate from the old camera.

The pattern was undeniable. Certain people appeared in one set but not the other. The longer he stared, the more impossible it felt.

His hands trembled as he opened his laptop. Most of the cameras were still running. He toggled through feeds, noting the same three "dead zones" — always the same places: the church basement, the forest by the lake, and the alley behind the general store.

He typed, mind racing:
INVISIBLE WEREWOLF

Dozens of links exploded across the screen. Todd clicked through folklore, legends, and even Reddit threads. Most were garbage — urban myths, creepypasta, cosplay blogs.

He growled in frustration — then stopped.

A page titled "Silvering and the Soul" caught his eye.

He opened it.

"Silvering is the process of applying a reflective coating to glass. In mirrors prior to the 19th century, tin and mercury were used to create a true reflection. These mirrors were believed to reveal not just images, but essence."

"In folklore, beings without souls cast no reflection — not due to invisibility, but incompatibility. Their essence does not register."

Todd typed again, faster now:
MIRROR SILVERING WEREWOLF
Then: **CAMERA MIRRORS SILVER**

Then: **VAMPIRE LEGENDS SILVER GLASS**

Another page opened — this one older, scanned from a book.

"In certain legends, vampires and other soul-bound creatures do not appear in reflections or photographs. Their spiritual energy does not imprint on silver-based mediums."

Todd leaned back slowly, a sick realization crawling over his spine.

These photos… they're not just pictures. They're filters. And whatever this is — whatever they are — they're not visible through silver.

He looked at the pile of photos again, this time with different eyes.

Then he whispered:

"They're not just vanishing from sight.
They were never supposed to be seen."

Chapter Twelve

Todd's eyes burned from hours without sleep. His fingers trembled slightly as he pinned the latest batch of glossy photos to the wall. The room had transformed into a chaotic crime lab—printouts, Polaroids, and handwritten notes sprawled across the once-blank walls. Red string connected key faces, locations, and timestamps like veins of madness spiderwebbing out from a single word.

With a thick black marker, Todd scrawled **VAMPIRES** in bold, aggressive strokes across the center of the board. The ink bled slightly into the drywall, but he didn't care. He dropped the marker onto his bed and exhaled slowly, surveying his work.

He'd printed out every scrap of evidence he could find, local legends buried in forgotten forums, crime reports that quietly mentioned bite marks, a blurry image of a pale face caught in the woods at night. The evidence was old, yet the faces in the photos weren't. One article, decades old, told the story of a settler family drained of blood during the town's founding. Another was an obituary with a photo of someone who looked eerily like Jack, dated 1947.

The air in the room felt stale, metallic. Todd's head throbbed.

"What the hell is this place?" he muttered.

He rubbed his eyes, trying to blink away the gritty exhaustion. For a moment, the photos seemed to shift—faces appearing closer or farther than they should, expressions subtly rearranging themselves. He told himself it was the lack of sleep. Nothing more.

From the hall, the house was still. Too still. Todd swallowed, ears straining. No clatter of dishes from the kitchen. No creaking floorboards from George pacing while thinking. Not even the faint hum of the TV, George always left on as background noise. Just a heavy, suffocating quiet.

He stepped into the living room, eyes drifting toward the darkened kitchen, the hallway, the front door. The air was colder out here. The thermostat glowed on the wall, but the number didn't match what he felt on his skin.

"Dad?" Todd called out, voice low but urgent. No response.

The silence pressed back.

A strange chill curled up his spine as he stared at the front door. He moved toward it, hand hovering over the knob, imagining—ridiculously but vividly—that something waited on the other side. Something breathing. Something listening.

Just then, keys jingled outside, sharp and bright against the quiet. The lock turned.

Todd flung the door open before the knob finished twisting.

There stood George—and behind him, Maria. Both froze, surprised to see Todd standing in the frame like he'd been waiting for them.

"Where have you been?" George snapped. "I've been calling you all morning."

Todd rubbed the back of his neck, eyes darting to their faces. Maria's cheeks were flushed like she'd been laughing. George looked slightly disheveled, jacket unbuttoned, hair wind-tossed.

"We built a darkroom in the basement," Todd said. "I guess I fell asleep down there."

Maria slipped inside and headed for the couch without saying a word. She carried herself with that same eerie grace she always had—too smooth, too controlled. She sat, legs crossed, watching Todd with unreadable eyes. There was something predatory in the stillness of her posture.

George busied himself in the kitchen, rifling through drawers like he was searching for something he'd misplaced. His tone stayed casual. "So? Did you develop anything useful?"

Todd moved to the edge of the living room, leaning against the hallway doorframe. "Yeah. Some of it's blurry... but some of it's not."

Maria arched an eyebrow. "Still playing detective?"

Todd didn't answer right away. His gaze drifted to her hands—perfectly still on her knee. Not a twitch. Not a fidget. People were never that still.

"The more I look," he said slowly, "the less sense it makes. This town's like... fake. Or hollow. Like a film set someone forgot to take down."

Maria smirked. "Maybe you're just bored."

George reappeared with a bottle of wine. The label was dusty, as if it had been tucked away and forgotten for years.

"Or maybe he's losing his mind," George said cheerfully.

Maria reached for the bottle, fingers brushing George's. Their moment lingered too long. Todd caught it, his jaw tightening.

"Got the wine," George said. "Let's go."

"Where?" Todd asked, though he already knew he wouldn't like the answer.

George didn't answer. Maria moved toward the door, fluid like a shadow.

Todd stepped forward and grabbed George's arm—not roughly, but with urgency. "What about the case? What about the missing people, the attacks?"

George's eyes narrowed. "The town's not going anywhere. Neither are we. So why don't you slow down and take a breath? We'll talk more tonight."

Maria touched George's arm. "Let's not keep the Mayor waiting."

Todd froze. "You're meeting with him again?"

George pulled free. "Don't start."

They stepped out onto the porch and closed the door behind them.

Todd stood there in the quiet afterward, hands balled into fists. The sound of their footsteps faded down the street far too quickly, swallowed by the still air. Something felt wrong—wrong with them, wrong with the house, wrong with the whole damn town.

After a long beat, he returned to his room, slamming the door shut.

He paced like a caged animal. His eyes landed on a photo of Matthew and the Mayor entering the church. He yanked a sticky note off his desk, scribbled **STARTING HERE**, and slapped it onto the corner of the picture.

He stared at the wall a moment longer, as if waiting for the photos to speak. They didn't. But something in the back of his mind whispered anyway.

He grabbed his jacket, stuffed his camera into a messenger bag, and left the house.

Outside, Pine Lakes felt... hollow. As he trudged through town, he noticed Main Street was unusually empty, as if the whole town had taken a collective nap. No cars. No chatter. Not even a bird cutting across the sky. The flags on the lamp posts hung completely still, as if even the air refused to move.

The sun pressed low in the sky, casting long shadows across the storefronts. Todd's footsteps echoed louder than usual, bouncing off empty windows and brick walls like someone—or something—was following just behind him, out of sight.

He walked fast, eyes flicking from building to building. His mind buzzed with theories—secret tunnels, underground rituals, ancient bloodlines, hypnotism. The town felt like it was holding its breath.

A sudden voice jolted him out of his thoughts.

"Hey, stranger. What are you up to?"

Todd flinched so hard he nearly tripped over the curb. He spun around.

Sandra stood behind him, smiling warmly, arms folded across her chest.

"Jesus," he breathed. "I'm going to die of a heart attack before I figure any of this out."

She stepped closer, amused. "Sorry. Didn't mean to sneak up on you." Her expression softened. "You okay?"

"Define okay," Todd said as he rubbed his face.

She studied him for a moment, frown lines softening into concern. "You look like you haven't slept in a week."

"Feels like it."

Sandra tilted her head. "Are you still coming on that boat ride tonight?"

Todd considered it. The idea was tempting—escape, drugs, Sandra—but the urgency clawing at his insides was louder, pulsing, insistent.

"Maybe," he said. "You're a good time... and I do like drugs."

Sandra gave him a sly look. "That sounds like a yes."

Todd hesitated, then asked, "Have you seen my dad?"

She nodded. "Just saw him down by the docks. With Maria… and the Mayor."

Todd's stomach dropped. "Of course he was."

Sandra's brows knit. "What's going on?"

He was already backing away. "I'll tell you later."

Sandra watched him break into a jog, then a sprint. The breeze caught her hair as she stood alone in the middle of the empty street, watching him disappear into the distance.

All around her, the town seemed to exhale—soft, faint, like something shifting beneath the earth. Somewhere behind the buildings, a dog—or something that only sounded almost like a dog—howled once, long and low.

Sandra turned slowly and began walking the other direction, the echo of that howl chasing her until it faded… or until something else answered.

Chapter Thirteen

Todd stood frozen on the front lawn of the old church, his heartbeat pounding louder than the wind whispering through cracked stone and peeling paint. The once-majestic building loomed before him like a forgotten relic, its stained-glass windows fractured and dulled by decades of neglect. Even in daylight, it radiated an ominous chill—as if it were watching him just as he was watching it.

He swallowed hard, a cold sweat trickling down his neck, and took a hesitant step forward. The worn stone steps creaked beneath his weight, their echoes swallowed by the heavy silence. Reaching the heavy wooden door, he grasped the iron handle—and to his surprise, it swung open with a low, reluctant groan.

The main hall inside was a cavern of dust and shadows. Pale sunlight filtered through colored glass, scattering broken rainbows across cracked plaster walls and long-abandoned pews. Todd's camera clicked softly as he documented the beauty of decay, the shutter echoing the loneliness of the place —spiderwebs draped like curtains, dust glittering in thin beams of light, silence heavy as a shroud.

His fingers trailed along the back of a pew, stirring up a fine cloud of dust, when something caught his eye—a trail of faint footprints imprinted in the thick layer of grime. The prints led toward the far end of the hall, where a heavy set of cellar doors sat partially concealed in shadow.

Todd's breath hitched. He crouched to examine the footprints more closely—human-sized, uneven, as if the person had hurried. Slowly, carefully, he pulled the cellar doors open, revealing a narrow metal staircase descending into darkness.

Clutching his camera, Todd descended the stairs, each metallic step ringing out sharply in the stillness. At the bottom, he entered a long sterile corridor bathed in cold white light, its walls tiled with pale green doors at regular intervals. He lifted his camera and took a quick photo of the surreal scene, then tested each door…locked—all of them.

At the far end, Todd rapped sharply on the brick wall. The hollow echo was unnerving. Running his palm over the rough bricks, he felt a slight depression—almost imperceptible. His fingertip pressed it, and with a slow grinding noise, a concealed panel slid open, revealing a brightly lit laboratory beyond.

Todd's breath caught in his throat.

Rows of bodies hung suspended from the ceiling, each encased in translucent plastic sheaths. Tubes and wires connected them to machines humming softly with artificial life. Thick, dark liquid oozed through transparent tubes, disappearing into the floor below. The sight was grotesque yet mesmerizing—like something from a nightmare.

He raised his camera and began documenting, snapping photos of the hollow, pale faces pressed against the plastic. Their eyes stared blankly, as if trapped between life and death.

Suddenly, an elevator on the other side of the room pinged, its doors sliding open. The Mayor stepped out, his cold gaze locking onto Todd instantly.

Behind him padded the massive black wolf Todd had been hunting—its eyes gleaming with unnatural intelligence.

"Son of a bitch," Todd whispered.

"Hello, Todd," the Mayor said smoothly, stepping forward with a predator's grace.

Todd stumbled back, tripping over a cable and hitting the floor. The Mayor removed his jacket and hung it over one of the bodies like he owned the room. The wolf sat at his side, silent, waiting.

"Your father speaks highly of you," the Mayor said, voice low and chilling. "I doubted him. But here you are."

Todd forced himself to his feet, raising his camera. "My dad hasn't said a good word about me in years. Cut the bullshit."

The Mayor crouched, running a hand over the wolf's thick fur. "I want things to be different, Todd. You're a survivor. I knew it the moment we met."

"Don't let that fool you," Todd shot back. "Now tell me what's really going on."

A thin, cruel smile twisted the Mayor's lips. "In all my years, I've never met anyone immune to the gift we have here. Until recently. I faced a challenge."

He gestured to the wolf. "Many gifts lie hidden in this world."

Todd frowned. "What?"

"He was dying," the Mayor said, pacing slowly, tossing objects aside without care. "His family tried everything—medicine, prayers, nothing worked. In return for their service." He waved his hands at the bodies suspended in the air. "I saved him."

The wolf shuddered violently, bones cracking and reshaping under the surface as the creature transformed—dropping fur, sinew, and teeth—until standing before Todd was a naked, glistening Ernie coated in a slick slime. His eyes held shame and fear.

"Sorry, man," Ernie whispered.

Without warning, the Mayor lunged, grabbing Todd by the throat with terrifying strength.

"Survival is a business, Todd," he hissed. "If you don't want to join us, then I can't let you leave."

He threw Todd hard down the hallway. Todd's body slammed against the cold tile, sliding toward the staircase. Struggling to stand, he glanced back— The Mayor advancing, Ernie following, donning a hastily thrown-on lab coat.

Adrenaline surged as Todd bolted up the stairs, bursting through the cellar door into the sun-filled room. He ran for the front doors, and suddenly they opened— Sandra stepped in, flanked by three others.

He spun back the way he came, relief hit him, then vanished when Ernie emerged from the cellar behind him.

"I told my dad this place was screwed up," Todd muttered, edging cautiously between the pews, putting distance between himself and the group.

Sandra's voice was calm, reverent. "This was where it began. Humanity was dying. We just… took what they no longer deserved."

She advanced slowly, flanked by her friends, forcing Todd to crawl over the pews to evade them. Todd scoffed bitterly. "Hematologist, huh? I get it now. That's funny."

Sandra's expression softened, concern flashing in her eyes. "I need you to take this seriously."

Todd twisted away, dodging their advances. "Seriously? Up until a few days ago, vampires and werewolves were stories—myths. How am I supposed to take this seriously?"

"You said you wanted to show the world what they're missing," Sandra said quietly. "It's right here."

They locked eyes. Todd is now unknowingly standing over the cellar stairs.

"Join us," she whispered. "Help reveal the truth."

Todd's expression hardened. "I can't."

His smile faltered, but before he could react, the Mayor moved like a blur, his hand bursting through Todd's chest in a grotesque, unnatural movement.

 The Mayor pulled him close in a cruel and possessive embrace. He slung his head back, fangs flashing, then sinking into Todd's neck, tearing flesh as blood streamed down. Todd's hands clenched tightly, trembling with shock. The Mayor sank his teeth into Todd's neck one last time with animalistic hunger.

Sandra stood frozen as The Mayor withdrew his arm from Todd's chest, letting his limp body slump to the floor. Turning to Sandra, the Mayor raised his bloodied hand and slid his thumb into her mouth. She tasted Todd's blood as he pressed a dark kiss on her forehead.

Without a word, he disappeared back into the cellar.

Ernie sat nearby on a pew, his cold gaze fixed on Sandra as he spoke in a low voice.

"You knew this was how it would end."

Sandra said nothing as Ernie stood and walked away, leaving the church steeped in silence and the heavy scent of blood.

Chapter Fourteen

George and Maria sat on the pontoon boat, the last colors of the sunset bleeding into the lake like bruises. The surface rippled gently, disturbed only by the fading wake of passing ducks and the occasional splash of a fish. An empty wine bottle leaned sideways beside Maria's crossed legs, its cork bobbing just beneath the boat's edge. A napkin fluttered in the breeze, skimming the deck before catching on George's boot.

Maria leaned her head on his shoulder, her voice barely above a whisper. "I used to think this place was a dream."

George gave a soft grunt of agreement, wrapping an arm around her. "Still might be," he said. "Just one of those dreams you don't know is a nightmare till it's too late."

They sat in silence, letting the night settle around them like a heavy quilt. Crickets chirped in the distance.

As the stars emerged, they walked hand in hand down the road back toward the Webb house. Streetlights buzzed lazily above them, casting elongated shadows. Maria kicked at a rock, sending it skittering across the road.

"You ever wish you hadn't come here?" she asked.

George gave it a moment. "I go where the universe guides me; this time it sent me where I belong."

At the porch steps, George slowed. "Do you mind hanging out while I go over some stuff with Todd?" Maria nodded. "Of course. I don't have anywhere else to be."

George offered her a quiet smile. "He's... the way he is because I've ignored him so long. I think he just needs to know someone gives a damn."

Maria touched his arm gently. "Then go show him."

Inside, the house felt colder than expected. Still. No music, no flickering screen, no telltale thuds from Todd's room. George walked into the kitchen and opened the fridge, grabbing a beer more for comfort than thirst. The click and hiss of the bottle opening was too loud in the stillness.

"Kid?" he called. No answer.

He checked the living room and the hallway. Nothing. When he reached Todd's room, the door creaked slightly as he pushed it open. The bed was made. The air is stale. The only signs of life were the flurry of photos taped to the walls.

George stepped inside, tension creeping up his spine. He dialed Todd's number. Voicemail.

"Where are you at, kid?" he murmured, dropping down onto the edge of the bed. "I came home to go over your damn photos. Don't make me chase you."

He stared up at the ceiling, then over to the collage of pinned photos. His eyes were drawn to a messy scrawl across several of them. The word **VAMPIRE** circled in thick marker stood out like a scream. A picture of Matthew—eyes wide and dead, blood pooling beneath him—stared back from one corner. The gruesome image made George's stomach twist.

He moved closer. More photos were layered beneath the visible ones, half-hidden like secrets. A note fluttered to the floor as he pulled one free. Todd's handwriting read:

"STARTING HERE."

It was pinned over a photo of the church's steeple. Beside it, an older film photo showed George and the Mayor—except the developed print only displayed George. The space where The Mayor should be was washed out, blank.

George ran a hand through his hair, heart thumping. "No. No no no... What the hell is all this?"

A soft electronic beep echoed from Todd's backpack. George darted to it and unzipped it. The laptop was warm. He flipped it open just in time to see a low battery warning blink out.

"Shit," he muttered, searching wildly. A power cord was half-lodged beneath the bed. He yanked it out and plugged the laptop in.

The screen came alive—dozens of GoPro windows lined up, each with timestamped feeds. Static on a few. Others showed views from high corners of buildings, rooftops, and hidden bushes. Todd had wired the whole town.

"You've been busy, kid," George said under his breath, scrolling through them.

One window caught his attention—the church steps. The Mayor stood there in silence, face calm but eyes hollow. He looked directly at the hidden camera nestled in a tree.

Then, slowly, he reached forward, locked his gaze with the lens—and smiled.

In one sudden motion, he ripped the device from its hiding spot. The screen went black.

George recoiled. "Of course, you've gone and pissed him off."

He began tearing photos from the walls, stacking maps and papers into Todd's duffel. Notes on missing persons, assets left behind, and old census pages with names crossed out. Everything pointed to a cover-up deeper than anything George had ever imagined.

In the living room, Maria had been flipping through a folder left on the coffee table. She glanced up as George entered. "Did you find anything?"

George dropped the files onto the table. "Depends on how you feel about vampires."

Maria didn't flinch. She spread the papers across the surface, eyes darting between images.

"You're not just here writing a book, are you?" she asked softly.

George shook his head. "Nope."

Maria leaned on the table, piecing together what Todd had uncovered. "How many people?"

"A lot," George admitted, voice cracking slightly. "Too many."

She studied him. "And you've been spending your time with me instead of following this?"

George looked down, guilty. "I didn't want to ruin whatever this is. Whatever we are."

Maria stepped in close, brushing a finger down his jaw. "I like you being here, George."

George nodded solemnly. "Todd's in danger. I can feel it."

He held up the note Todd had left. **STARTING HERE.**

Maria took it from him and read it silently.

"He wanted you to follow," she said.

George's voice was low but firm. "I have to."

A beat passed. Then—

"I'm coming with you," Maria said.

George looked at her, startled. "It might get dangerous. I mean it. Whatever this is—it's not normal."

Maria's expression hardened, but her voice remained calm. "I've lived here for nearly five years. I know how strange this town is. If you're walking into it, you're not doing it alone."

He nodded, finally accepting it.

Chapter Fifteen

The church rose out of the night like a wound stitched shut, a silhouette of rot and rumor under a slow, cold moon. Its stone face sagged; the steeple leaned as if tired of watching. George and Maria stood on the weed-choked lawn, the air between them full of something that tasted like iron. Even the insects stayed silent, as if the building itself swallowed sound.

Maria rolled a rusted key on a thin finger. "They've been 'restoring' this place for years," she said. "Donald said the foundation was bad. Said it would cost more than the town could ever raise."

George squinted up at the bowed roofline. "And nobody thought that was odd? In Alabama, a church doesn't just rot. People fix churches."

She shrugged—small, practiced. "People here waited. Maybe they wanted it to fall."

George didn't like the way she said that. Not scared. Not confused. Almost... resigned.

He studied her face. "You really never wondered why?"

"For a while," she admitted. "But wondering in Pine Lakes is its own kind of danger."

Something tightened in George's chest. A flicker of doubt. A crack in trust. He didn't know why, but the way she stood—close, but not too close—made him feel like the two of them were already on opposite sides of something he hadn't yet learned.

She stepped forward and slipped the key into the lock. The old door groaned like a wounded animal as it swung open. A sudden gust of stale air blasted from the sanctuary, thick with mildew and ash. Dust swirled in slow spirals, catching moonlight in strange, weightless patterns. The smell was wrong—too cold, like something buried deep underground had been let out to breathe.

They stepped into a sanctuary where the air inside was frigid, unmoving. Pews lay crooked, like broken teeth in a forgotten mouth. The altar, once sacred, was draped in cobwebs and flanked by extinguished candelabras. A bible lay open on the floor, its pages warped by moisture and blackened at the edges, as if burned from the inside out.

George took a cautious step forward, the wood creaking beneath his boots. Maria stopped abruptly. "Oh," she whispered—thin, sharp, almost choked.

Ahead, near the altar, three children knelt in a circle — their backs to the door, heads bowed like tiny monks. Between them lay Todd.

He was still as a broken doll, pale as winter, blood dark and thick across his shirt, a pool collecting beneath him. The children leaned close, sipping from his wounds with slow, ritual precision—an awful ceremony performed in silence, as natural to them as breathing.

George's world narrowed to a single point.

He stumbled forward and fell to his knees beside his son. The children scattered like frightened animals, disappearing behind pews and pillars. Todd's body was cold and hollow beneath George's shaking hands.

"Please," George croaked. "No. Not him."

A voice came from the dark—soft, almost gentle. "I'm so sorry."

They turned toward the sound.

Sandra stepped from the shadowed aisle, face half-lit by moonlight, her eyes too calm to be human. Behind her, five figures shifted—seated like judges watching a verdict unfold.

George looked at Maria, desperation clawing through him. She didn't meet his eyes.

"Did you know?" he asked, voice breaking.

Sandra smiled—thin, knowing. "Of course she knew." She took a slow step forward, her heels whispering on the wood. "Maria was our guardian. Our protector. The little witch who kept Pine Lakes safe from outsiders and their questions."

George stared at Maria, the floor falling out beneath him. "What the hell is she talking about?"

Maria's lips trembled. "George—"

Sandra cut her off, voice rising in mock sermon. "She swore an oath long before you came sniffing around. The barrier holds only as long as she tends the old ways—salt, blood, silence. She grows tired. Still human and forgetting her prayers, letting the cracks widen."

Sandra's gaze drifted to Todd's lifeless body. "And through those cracks, the hunger slipped in."

Maria's hand lifted, trembling. "I tried to fix it—"

Sandra's smile sharpened. "You tried too late."

A shadow moved on the balcony. A tall figure descended—a gaunt woman with white eyes and hands like vines. She slipped behind Maria and rested one hand on her shoulder—almost affectionate.

Sandra tilted her head. "The town remembers its debts, Maria. You were supposed to keep it clean. Now look."

George surged forward, fury breaking his paralysis. "You don't touch her!"

Sandra raised her hand, and George froze mid-step. Her voice turned solemn, ritualistic. "We don't burn pyres without ceremony."

The white-eyed woman tightened her hand around Maria's skull.

SNAP.

Maria's body collapsed like a marionette with its strings cut.

George's scream tore through the church, raw and animal. "You didn't have to do that!"

Sandra only smiled wider. "We did. Her neglect let the gate rot. Her death will seal it."

Something inside George fractured. He lunged, but a shape burst from the shadows and tackled him into a pew. Wood exploded beneath them. George rolled and slammed his attacker into a jagged beam. The figure convulsed, hissed—and turned to ash.

He stared at the dust trembling in his hands. "Jesus Christ."

Above him, the remaining figures glided forward—faces pale as candlelight.

George tore a strip from a pew cushion, wrapped it around a splintered beam, and sparked his lighter. The makeshift torch roared to life. The figures recoiled, hissing.

He shoved through the doors, the burning torch catching the frame. Flames bloomed eagerly across the dry wood.

Inside the sanctuary, Sandra stood perfectly still amid the fire, her eyes reflecting the blaze like twin suns. The others melted into shadow.

George didn't look back. He ran to his jeep and started it.

He drove home in blind panic, headlights trembling across the trees. His breath came in ragged bursts, the echo of Maria's death following like a second heartbeat.

Upon arriving home, he stumbled inside, slamming the door. Pain lanced through his back—he reached behind and found a wooden shard buried deep into his body.

He burst into the kitchen, pulling bottles out of boxes until he found rubbing alcohol. He slammed the bottle down and tore his shirt off. He poured it down his back and over his wounds. White fire seared his nerves. Gritting his teeth, he pulled the fragment out with pliers. Blood soaked the floor. He stapled the wound shut, a quick, sickening click-click-click, pressed duct tape over it, and collapsed. The doorbell rang.

"Ernie?" he rasped. Silence.

Then a voice: "I'm looking for Todd. Haven't heard from him since last night."

George limped to the door and peered through the glass. The porch was empty.

He locked it, then scrambled to a drawer and opened it. Inside—revolver, box of .22 rounds, labeled in Todd's handwriting: IN CASE OF HELL.

He loaded the gun, shaking.

He made his way into Todd's room only to find it torn apart. Photos ripped down—red string shredded from the wall. And there—standing among the wreckage—was Matthew, calm and smiling.

"Your kid was sharp," Matthew said. "He figured it out fast. But you—easily manipulated."

George leveled the gun. "Don't touch anything."

Matthew picked up a Risk piece. "Do you ever learn from the games you play?"

George struck him hard across the face. Bone cracked. Matthew staggered, laughing through blood.

"You blame me," he said. "But your son knew. He found what was hidden. He woke it up."

"I said don't touch the game," George growled.

Matthew tossed him the dice. "Roll. Let's see who wins this time."

George didn't. He fired the gun. Matthew fell, screaming, laughing, changing. His eyes turned black, his jaw elongating into a bestial grin. "You're not ready," he hissed.

George emptied the gun into him. The bullets barely slowed him.

"My turn," Matthew said. He grabbed George by the throat and hurled him through the bedroom window.

Chapter Sixteen

Glass exploded outward as George burst through the upstairs window, his scream lost to the night. He crashed onto the Webb house roof in a shower of splinters and dust, shingles scraping his back as he rolled toward the edge. For one terrifying second, his body dangled over the drop — air whistling beneath him — before his fingers caught the rusted gutter. It moaned under his weight but held.

He hung there, chest heaving, arms trembling, pain flaring in every nerve. The air tasted like iron and smoke. After a moment, he pulled himself back onto the roof and lay flat, gasping. His pulse hammered in his ears like a trapped bird.

 From the shattered window above, Matthew crawled out slow, deliberate, his torn skin already knitting itself closed, like something born wrong. His eyes glowed in the flicker of the broken light behind him, feral and hungry.

"I was scared at first," Matthew said softly. "They weren't nice to me. Not like they were to Todd. They gave him a chance."

George twisted on his side, watching him advance. The fog wrapped the roofline, turning the world into a smothered blur.

Matthew reached out and helped George to his feet — gentle, almost kind. He brushed the dust off George's shoulders as if they were old friends. The gesture made George's stomach turn.

"With me," Matthew continued, voice darkening, "Donald ate first. Told me about the side effects later."

Before George could answer, Matthew's hand clamped his chest and flung him off the roof.

George hit the ground with a sound like a car crash. The world vanished into pain. Fog swirled thick and alive, pressing against him as if it wanted him to stay down. His lungs burned; every movement felt underwater.

Next to him, Matthew landed in an animalistic crouch. His landing was thunder, scattering the fog and silencing the crickets. The backyard was bathed in the eerie yellow beam from the swaying shed light. It painted Matthew in strips of brightness and shadow. His skin looked bruised with veins. His lips peeled back to reveal fangs. He grinned, walking slowly—fingers twitching, joints popping as if something underneath the skin was trying to get out.

George forced himself upright, spitting blood. "All the missing people… where are they?"

Matthew's smile spread wide, cracking his face into something monstrous. "Everywhere." "They don't always stay here," Matthew said, stepping forward. His voice was smooth, detached. "Some leave. Some change. But they never really go."

George barely saw the movement before Matthew slammed him through the side of the shed. The impact shattered wood and bone alike. The hanging bulb inside swung wildly, casting stuttering light across George's bleeding face.

He staggered up, ribs screaming. Something metallic glinted near his hand.

Matthew's voice floated in. "You and your son — you'll just be another name."

George's hand found the ax. Its handle was old, splintered—but solid.

"They'll forget you," Matthew whispered. "Like they forgot the rest."

 He leaned through the hole, smiling. "You okay, buddy?"

George did not answer.

He was done listening.

He swung.

The ax split Matthew's jaw, spraying the shed walls in black blood. The creature staggered backward, shrieking. George followed, yanking the weapon free, twisting as Matthew stumbled into the yard.

For a heartbeat, everything slowed — the fog, the breath, the blood.

Then George brought the ax down again.

Matthew fell hard, his body twitching in the dirt. George's boot pressed against his chest as he wrenched the blade loose with a wet crack.

But the body didn't stay still. The air rippled, vibrating with a strange hum. Matthew's face began to re-form — bones sliding back into place, skin knitting together like paper healing in reverse.

George didn't think. He swung again.

And again.

On the third blow, the ax sank deep, severing the head from the body. The corpse shuddered once and then disintegrated into a burst of dry ash, carried off by the wind.

George dropped to his knees, chest heaving. His hands shook. He could taste the ash on his tongue.

The fog around him began to move.

He turned. Three figures stalked from the mist. Jack. A woman with hollowed-out sockets. A man with blood staining his chin. They were spectral, half there and half not. Their bodies flickered at the edges, like tape left too long in the sun. Their eyes glowed. Their mouths opened. Teeth slid down like knives.

George hurled the ax.

It struck Jack in the chest, driving him backward into the fog with a gurgling screech. The others rushed in.

George dove aside, rolling through the dirt, and landed near Jack. He grasped the handle, yanking hard. The axe head wouldn't budge, and the handle came right off. As George looked at the broken handle, confused, something grabbed him from behind and hurled him upward like a doll.

He hit the ground hard enough to see stars. The fog trembled. His ribs ground like glass.

Another creature pounced. Instinct took over. George jammed the broken ax handle upward — straight through its throat. The thing burst into ash mid-air. He gagged as the dust rained into his face.

The last vampire, Jack — the one with the ax still buried in its chest — crawled toward him, snarling.

George met it halfway.

It rolled through the wet grass, thrashing. George pinned him down and drove the broken handle into its chest again and again until it stopped moving, until it wasn't there anymore.

Silence fell. Only George's ragged breathing filled the night.

He knelt there, bloodied and shaking, barely human. His heartbeat slowed to something dark and heavy.

Then — a rustle.

A new shape in the fog.

Before he could react, an arm wrapped around his throat, fangs scraped skin. George choked, clawing at the attacker's face. He gripped its head with both hands and shoved hard.

It hissed.

His free hand found the jagged wood handle. He drove it upward, straight through the vampire's mouth.

They struggled — grunting, twisting, pulling against each other — until George heaved sideways, all his strength behind it.

The head tore free, and the body exploded into ash.

George rolled away, coughing, shaking. He lay there for a long moment, staring up at the gray sky, chest rising and falling in shallow bursts. The fog closed in again, soft and suffocating, like a shroud.

When he finally stood, his body ached in every direction. But something inside him had changed. His reflection would never look the same again.

The bite on his neck pulsed hot and deep.

He staggered toward the front yard, dragging the broken ax handle with him like a wounded knight returning from war.

Ernie sat on the porch, waiting calmly. George walked up the steps and stopped. He held the axe handle up to him.

"That won't do much to me, man," he said, smiling.

George gripped the handle tighter. "It killed everyone else. I think I can make it work."

Ernie rose slowly, eyes catching the dim light. "I'm not everyone else."

In a blink, he grabbed George and hurled him off the porch. George hit the ground hard, coughing blood.

"I'm better," Ernie growled, voice thickening. "I'm stronger."

He tore off his shirt. His skin rippled, twitching. Then he dropped to his knees and screamed — a sound that split the air in half.

Bones snapped. Muscles stretched. Fur erupted from his flesh in bursts. His spine cracked, bending backward.

George watched, frozen. "Son of a bitch…"

Ernie's mouth split open, reshaping into a muzzle. His eyes drowned in black.

Then came the howl.

Low. Endless. Inhuman.

George turned and ran. Limping. Dragging his blood and breath toward the Jeep.

He dove inside, slammed the door, and locked it.

Chapter Seventeen

George slammed the keys into the ignition and twisted. The Jeep choked, coughed—then roared awake just as a massive weight crashed onto the hood, caving in metal with a scream of twisting steel.

Wolf-Ernie landed in a crouch, no longer a man but something wrong. His torso was elongated, ribs showing through matted fur slick with blood and ash. His snout split open in a guttural snarl, drool stringing from teeth that didn't belong in any earthly jaw.

The creature struck its claws, punched through the windshield. Glass erupted inward like frozen rain. George jerked back and slammed the accelerator. The Jeep shot into reverse, tires spitting gravel.

Behind him, the fog lit red, glowing like something alive. Shapes moved within it, silhouettes with gleaming eyes, grinning teeth, long shadows stretching like hungry fingers.

Ernie slid off the hood with a wet thud. But others were faster.

One landed on the roof. Another crashed into the passenger door so hard the frame buckled.

Two smeared bloody hands across the shattered windshield, grinning wide enough to split their cheeks.

George twisted the wheel hard left, then right. The Jeep fishtailed violently. A vampire skidded off the roof, rolling bonelessly across the dirt. Another clung to the mirror, grinning inches from George's face until he jerked the wheel again and sent it spinning into the dark with a crunch.

The Jeep burst from the fog, rubber screaming on pavement.

 And there, standing in the middle of the street, was Sandra.

Still.

Waiting.

She wore the same clothes he remembered, now streaked with ash, like she had been expecting him all along.

"Shit!"

He jerked the wheel too late. The Jeep hit her. Her body flopped onto the hood lifelessly—
—until she moved.

She rose with unnatural flexibility, hooked a leg over the roof rail, and swung down like a gymnast. Her head dipped through the shattered passenger window, her arms folding insect-like as she slid into the seat beside him.

"Hi, Georgie," she purred, voice wet and broken. Her lips curled to reveal teeth lengthened into needles.

Her breath smelled like rot and sour wine.

"Your blood…" She inhaled deeply. "God, it smells divine."

Her jaw snapped. A hinge cracked loudly.

George didn't think—he just drove.

He floored it.

The Jeep screamed forward, engine howling as it barreled toward the ruined church. He never touched the brakes. The front end smashed into the stone steps with an earth-shaking boom, exactly the collision he had gambled on.

Sandra flew through what was left of the windshield like a rag doll. She hit the wall, slid down, and crumpled.

Smoke filled the cab. George shoved the buckled driver's door open and spilled onto the ground, hacking, dragging the ax handle after him.

The Jeep's hood caught fire. Flames licked up Sandra's legs.

She stood. Fire consuming her hair, her clothes, her skin, and she walked through it unfazed.

She lunged.

George swung. He drove the ax handle into her temple with a sickening crack, pinning her head to the stone wall. Flames devoured her from the inside. She screamed before bursting into a cyclone of ash.

It snowed down on George, sticking to his cuts and sweat.

He ripped the handle free and staggered back.

From the darkness behind him came a voice:

"Buddy… what are you doing to my town?"

George turned.

The Mayor stood on the top step of the church. Hands folded like a disappointed father watching a child ruin a toy.

"What am I doing?" George shouted, shaking. "What the fuck am I doing?!"

"We treated you with hospitality," the Mayor said, descending each step deliberately. "We gave you room. Community. A place for your boy." His voice held genuine injury. "And in return, you burn our buildings and butcher my citizens."

"You killed my son!" George's voice cracked raw.

The Mayor didn't blink. "He was curious. Too curious. He trespassed."

Rage snapped through George. He stepped forward.

The Mayor gestured toward the church doors. "Come. There's something you need to see."

Inside, smoke pooled thick in the rafters. Charred pews were filled with figures—silent, watching. Their eyes glowed red in the gloom, dozens of them tracking George like prey entering a den.

A low hum vibrated through the floorboards. Breathing. Or chanting. Or both.

The Mayor walked up to the pulpit.

"Then I looked," he intoned, voice echoing through the ruins, "and behold—a pale horse. Its rider's name was Death. And Hades followed with him…"

George walked the center aisle, every step heavier than the last.

"…They were given power over a fourth of the earth," the Mayor continued, "to kill by sword, famine, plague… and the beasts of the earth."

George spat. "Beasts. That's what you are."

The Mayor smiled thinly. "We are what human nature always intended."

George swallowed. "Do you have a god?"

"Don't we all?" the Mayor said. He slid aside a burnt tapestry, revealing a descending stairwell. He gestured. "Ours simply hungers differently."

George hesitated.

The Mayor leaned close. "You will leave this place in one of two ways: torn apart by my flock behind you… or peacefully, as someone willing to understand."

Then he turned and descended.

George followed. The stairwell gave way to cold stone. Heat vanished. Air sharpened. White tile replaced charred wood. The hallway stretched long and sterile, lined with green metal doors.

Everyone locked.
Everyone trembling faintly—like something inside was shifting.

At the end stood a blank white panel.

"What is this?" George asked.

The Mayor placed his palm against the wall. A hiss. A mechanical groan. The stone split apart.

The smell hit first—sour, metallic, rotting.

Inside hung bodies.
Dozens.
Upside down like livestock.
Drained.
Pale.
Some still twitching.

George stumbled back.

"Your son found this place," the Mayor said quietly. "Sharp kid. Would've made a hell of a journalist."

"If you hadn't murdered him…" George whispered.

"You don't walk into a man's house and open his doors without permission," the Mayor replied. "That isn't civility."

George tightened his grip on the ax handle.

He wasn't getting out of this peacefully.
And they both knew it.

Chapter Eighteen

The laboratory beneath the church was colder than George expected—an unnatural, clinical chill that bit through his soaked clothes and numbed the blood already caking on his skin. The sterile tile floor stretched out before him like a morgue's welcome mat, each of his steps echoing off steel walls and flickering fluorescent bulbs that buzzed like angry insects.

Bodies hung from meat hooks along the walls—men, women, some barely recognizable as human. Some twitched. Others gurgled quietly. Many didn't move at all.

George stepped cautiously, every sense tuned for motion, breath fogging in the frigid air.

The Mayor strolled between the bodies, hands folded behind his back, like a man inspecting artwork. His voice was soft, nearly paternal.

"We've turned survival into a business," he said, gesturing at the grotesque spectacle. "You can't imagine what it takes to keep a place like this running."

George's grip on the blood-slick ax handle tightened until his knuckles cracked. "My son wanted to tear it down."

The Mayor didn't look back. "Yes. And you want to finish what he started." He chuckled, low and dry. "You think you're the first person to show up and cause trouble?"

He vanished into the shadows between bodies.

"There've been so many…"

George turned in place, trying to follow the voice, which now echoed from all sides like a mocking ghost. The shifting light warped the edges of the lab, stretching the walls, bending the space until it felt like the room itself was breathing.

Then, cold hands gripped his throat.

George was yanked backward, feet lifted off the ground. The Mayor's eyes gleamed with red malice as he lifted George with one hand, his strength inhuman.

"You know the hardest part of all this?" the Mayor asked. His breath was warm and foul against George's cheek.

George wheezed, barely able to whisper. "Do… tell…"

"We could've been great friends."

George let out a broken laugh; the idea was so grotesque it almost sobered him.

Then the Mayor hurled him like a discarded puppet. George smashed into a metal shelf lined with IV bags. They exploded in crimson waves, drenching him in blood that was hot and thick and suffocating.

He gasped and choked, clawing his way out of the puddle, hands flailing for the ax.

The Mayor approached slowly, savoring the moment. He crouched beside George and dragged a long, slow tongue across his cheek. "I don't have many friends."

George laughed through his coughs, blood and spit trailing from his mouth.

The Mayor hesitated, puzzled by the defiance.

George saw the opening with the instinct of a man who had already made peace with dying.

That second was all George needed.

With a grunt, he rammed the ax handle into the side of the Mayor's head. A sickening crunch echoed through the chamber. The Mayor shrieked—a high, fractured sound not meant for human ears—and reeled backward, clawing at the shaft protruding from his skull.

George scrambled to his feet, slipping in the blood but pushing forward. The Mayor flailed, smashing into machines, knocking over trays of tools and bone saws.

George spotted the elevator.

The Mayor did too.

As the wounded creature scrambled toward the call button, George launched himself forward with a primal roar.

The elevator doors opened just as he tackled the Mayor. The two men slammed inside, the force of the impact rattling the walls.

George straddled the Mayor's chest and yanked the ax handle free. He raised it and brought it down into the Mayor's neck—again. And again.

With each brutal blow, the elevator jolted like a boat in a storm. Blood painted the walls and mirrored ceiling.

George didn't stop until the Mayor's head tore free with a final wet snap. The body convulsed once—then collapsed into a heap of black ash.

Silence fell.

George slumped forward, gasping. His reflection above was unrecognizable—hair plastered to his face, blood in his eyes, every inch of him broken or bruised.

Then the elevator dropped, and the crash came like thunder.

When it finally stopped, the doors buckled, dented just enough for George to pry them open and crawl out.

He emerged into a red-lit corridor lined with pulsating tubes that glowed faintly like arteries. The air was warmer here, humid and metallic, like a butcher's breath. He staggered forward, hand on the wall, following the veined hallway.

It widened into a cave, and what a cave it was. Bones adorned the walls like cathedral stonework—skulls carefully arranged in rows, ribs bundled in grim wreaths. This was no tunnel of escape. It was a tomb—a sanctum.

Two robed figures stood guard at the threshold. They turn to the sound of anger echoing through the walls.

George didn't hesitate. He struck first—vicious, animalistic. The ax handle broke one's jaw in a single swing; the second went down with a crushed skull. They hit the ground like bags of meat bursting into dust.

At the center of the cavern stood a throne carved from twisted roots and bones. It was alive with black veins. A figure sat upon it—neither man nor beast, its body gaunt and leathery, like a mummy fed through a meat grinder.

Dozens of tubes ran from the walls into its back, suspended from the ceiling like puppet strings. It stirred as George approached, and then it rose. The movement was unnatural—mechanical, jerky. The tubes pulled taut as it stepped forward, limbs moving on delay, driven by something other than sinew and thought.

George raised the ax handle at him.

The ancient creature sniffed the air and turned its ruined face toward him. Its black eyes locked onto the stake.

Then—too fast to process—it lunged.

It grabbed George's wrist and shattered the bone with a sickening pop. He screamed, the pain blinding, but the creature only smiled.

With its other hand, it clutched his face and leaned close, breath like spoiled milk.

George, gritting his teeth, reached up with his remaining arm and yanked a cluster of tubes from the creature's back.

A howl exploded from its lungs.

Blood—thicker than tar—gushed from its spine.

The creature staggered.

George dropped to the floor beside the ax handle

He grabbed it.

Pulled himself up.

And rammed the stake into the creature's chest

It screamed.

He drove it in deeper—again—until the stake punched through its back and out the other side.

The body erupted in a geyser of ash and boiling blood. The blast hurled George across the cave like a doll. He slammed into the wall, hit the floor, and lay still.

He woke—alive somehow, but barely.

The once-mighty underground temple was a heap of shattered stone. Above him, the burning church blazed like a dying sun. Across the collapsed chamber, a narrow opening reflected a pale glow that looked almost like moonlight.

With everything else buried or burning, George chose the only path left.

He staggered into the tunnels—through shafts, through sewers—his mind slipping in and out of consciousness, hallucinations bleeding into memory as he pushed on.

Eventually, the stone gave way to concrete. The red glow faded. He saw a door.

He pushed through.

It opened into a maintenance shed behind the church. The outside world hit him like a slap—smoke, flame, the roar of fire. The church was ablaze, the Jeep fire having spread, engulfing everything in righteous destruction.

George turned back into the shed, grabbed a broken shovel, and smashed its head against the wall until it was jagged and sharp.

A final stake.

One more.

He limped across the front lawn, silhouetted by fire, dragging the stake behind him like a blade.

Then—movement.

A growl.

Ernie leapt from the darkness, fully transformed. Fur streaked with soot, jaws wide, eyes like red coals. He was no longer a man. He was hunger.

George turned, but too slowly.

The werewolf hit him like a missile.

They went down together.

Claws ripped. Fangs tore.

George screamed.

And the town of Pine Lakes watched silently from their porches, their windows, their doorsteps.

Hungry.

Alive.

And ready to begin again.

Dedication

For Todd Webb.

A bright light in a dark world.

Always missed.

www.ingramcontent.com/pod-product-compliance
Lightning Source LLC
Chambersburg PA
CBHW040148160726
48006CB00014B/1658